'A beautifully written story of grief and friendship woven through with myth and the power of the landscape. It won't leave my head.' PATRICE LAWRENCE

'Berlie Doherty is a   ID

'Mesmerising story   ?,
in a Jane Gardam   ghosts and hills
and folklore.' HILARY MCKAY

'*The Haunted Hills* effortlessly weaves the contemporary with the timeless. It's a reminder of the truth concealed in folklore – that our individual lives are just another chapter in the story of everyone. This book will haunt you, though you won't want it any other way.' THOMAS TAYLOR

'*The Haunted Hills* is a book that will entrance all who read it. A masterpiece.' KEVIN COBANE

'Full of atmosphere and hauntingly told, Doherty's words transport the reader to the mist covered hills where the past helps to reveal the truth of the present.' GILL LEWIS

'A gripping tale of fiery childhood friendship, loss and healing. Elegantly written, hugely atmospheric.' JULIAN SEDGWICK

'This most beautifully written novel turns on friendship, terrible loss and healing, and it's as tough-minded as it is moving.' KEVIN CROSSLEY-HOLLAND

HAVE YOU EVER WONDERED HOW BOOKS ARE MADE?

UCLan Publishing is an award winning independent publisher specialising in Children's and Young Adult books. Based at The University of Central Lancashire, this Preston-based publisher teaches MA Publishing students how to become industry professionals using the content and resources from its business; students are included at every stage of the publishing process and credited for the work that they contribute.

The business doesn't just help publishing students though. UCLan Publishing has supported the employability and real-life work skills for the University's Illustration, Acting, Translation, Animation, Photography, Film & TV students and many more. This is the beauty of books and stories; they fuel many other creative industries! The MA Publishing students are able to get involved from day one with the business and they acquire a behind the scenes experience of what it is like to work for a such a reputable independent.

The MA course was awarded a Times Higher Award (2018) for Innovation in the Arts and the business, UCLan Publishing, was awarded Best Newcomer at the Independent Publishing Guild (2019) for the ethos of teaching publishing using a commercial publishing house. As the business continues to grow, so too does the student experience upon entering this dynamic Masters course.

www.uclanpublishing.com
www.uclanpublishing.com/courses/
uclanpublishing@uclan.ac.uk

With love to all my family

The Haunted Hills is a uclanpublishing book

First published in Great Britain in 2022 by
uclanpublishing
University of Central Lancashire
Preston, PR1 2HE, UK

Text copyright © Berlie Doherty, 2022
Illustrations copyright © Tamsin Rosewell, 2022

978-1-912979-93-6

1 3 5 7 9 10 8 6 4 2

The right of Berlie Doherty and Tamsin Rosewell to be identified as the author
and illustrator of this work has been asserted in accordance with the
Copyright, Designs and Patents Act 1988.

Set in 10/16pt Kingfisher by Becky Chilcott.

A CIP catalogue record for this book is available from the British Library.

Printed and bound in Great Britain by Clays Ltd, Elcograf S.p.A.

BERLIE DOHERTY

The Haunted Hills

uclanpublishing

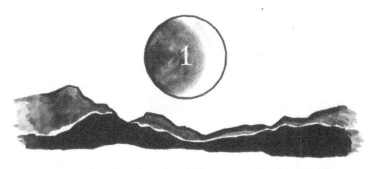

BEYOND THE BACK
OF BEYOND

I DIDN'T KNOW ANYWHERE COULD BE SO LONELY AS this dump of a cottage. How did people ever live in places like this, miles from anywhere? No TV, no internet, even now. Beyond the back of beyond, Dad calls it, but he likes it that way. The only other building anywhere in sight is the farmhouse at the end of a long stony track. I can just about see the roof and the chimney from Mum and Dad's room, and to do that I have to crouch down and squint through a tiny window. I can see the farmer's red tractor trundling down the track, spewing up dust because it's not even a proper road. All I can hear is the grumble of that tractor, and the sheep yelling to each other and coughing all day long. There's a bird endlessly twittering right high up in the sky. Gets on my nerves. And at night, outside it's as dark as a cave. I can't sleep because of the owls; they hoot for hours in a shivery, secretive sort of way, as if they're sending signals to one another. And the house creaks and groans as if somebody else is there, all the time. But especially at night. Especially in my room.

I feel stifled here. I never wanted to come in the first place, not after what happened. I don't need a holiday, Especially not here. I feel as if this cottage is some kind of prison, it's so dark and cold, even in broad daylight. We have to keep the light on all day and a wood fire burning, and it's nearly summer!

Mum loves it. She's prowling round the place like a hunting cat, taking photographs for her next exhibition, so she's not talking about much except light and shadows and lenses. As ever. Dad's just gone to see the farmer who owns the place about a leak in the kitchen. I'm twitchy with boredom, but out is better than in when there's no television and no internet anywhere. When there's nothing to do but think. And I don't want to think.

So, I decide to go for a walk.

I don't think there's anything to see, quite honestly. Except more hills, more fields, more stone walls. More sheep. But I quite like the idea of walking on my own, without Mum's chatter interrupting my thoughts, stealing my silences. And Dad has a way of forever pointing out things that he thinks might interest me – 'Look, Carl, a sheep's skull! Alas, poor Yorick, I knew him, Horatio' – as if I can't notice things for myself. He seems to think I have to be kept amused and interested. He wants to lift my spirits, as he keeps saying. But he tries too hard.

He's boring into my brain like a dentist's drill.

I'm walking blindly; I don't care where I'm going. I'm lost in some sort of gloomy trance, and I like being there. I squat down with my back against a mossy boulder. I close my eyes. If there's a view to look at, I don't bother. Sorry, Dad. Sometimes I find it hard not to think about what's going on inside my head. There's all kinds of stuff in there. Mostly about March 13th. I'm picking it over like a gull on a rubbish tip.

I should have been keeping an eye on where I was going. I'd thought that you could just climb up a hill, and then you walk down again and you're back where you started. It's not like that at all. There's no such thing as a straight line. Not on these scrubby moors. You have to keep avoiding boggy patches, heading for gaps in walls, tucking yourself away from sudden blasts of rainy winds. And when you turn round, everything looks the same anyway. So I'm lost.

What's more, I realise it's nearly dark. I'm a bit panicky now. It must be really late. I haven't a clue what time it is, or how long I've been out. My parents will be starting to worry. They'll be looking out for me, skittery as cats in case I've got hurt or done something stupid. They might even be thinking I've run away, tried to find my way home. Right now, I haven't a clue which direction I should be going in. Everywhere I look there's the same dim green grass, rocks, boulders, clumps of heather. I stagger down in what I think must be the right way and find nothing I recognise. I turn in another direction, and then another. I'm lost, completely lost. Night is falling fast. I don't want to be here, not on my own. I'm scared.

Now I think I see a figure coming towards me in the gloom. I can't tell; is somebody there, or am I imagining it? Is it my dad, come looking for me? I know it isn't though. Not tall enough;

too thin. I try to call out. My voice is catching in my throat. I'm suddenly scared. I don't know now whether anyone is there at all. Oh, but it is, surely, it's a boy. He's about my age, a bit taller than me, with a hat pulled down over his head. He has a dog at his side. He stops some distance away, just looking at me, as if he's trying to make me out too, as if he's afraid to come any nearer. I can't see his face.

'Take him home, Bob,' he says. I think he says that anyway. I can't tell if it's a voice or the wind. And then I can't see him any more. He's gone.

I don't know what's happening now. I don't know whether anyone is there or not. But the dog's here all right. It comes leaping towards me, barking and bobbing and dodging till I know he's trying to coax me as if I'm a stray sheep, making me turn round and walk in the opposite direction to the one I think I should be going in. What can I do? I have to trust him. He lollops around me, sometimes barking softly with a slight *yip! yip!* as if he's encouraging me. Now he runs ahead and stops, turns, and then he runs off again as soon as I reach him, until I'm going as fast as I can after him on that bumpy black hill and I'm tripping and stumbling, and at last below me I can see the distant glow of a house light, and I know it has to be the farm and that our holiday cottage is nearby. Then the dog just slopes away, disappearing into the darkness.

I can see a small, wavering light now, and I know it's the light of a torch. I run towards it, shouting, and soon I can hear Dad's voice shouting back.

'Carl? Carl? He's here, Louise! He's back!'

'Course I am!' I say, breathless with running.

Then Dad's there, grinning at me, and he claps me on the shoulder and leads me into the warmth of the cottage. The fire is glittering in the hearth; it's just been rekindled for me. 'Welcome home!' he says, trying to laugh it off, as if he hasn't been nearly out of his head with worry. Mum, tight-lipped, puts a plate of half-cold food on the table. I don't think she's angry. I think she's just too upset to say anything; she might burst into tears any minute.

I might too. But I'm back, I'm safe. I laugh it off with Dad. It's all a joke. Get some food down you. That's it. And I decide not to say anything about what just happened, and obviously they've decided the same. No questions. They're so protective of me just now, it won't do to tell them I was afraid up there, completely lost, scared out of my wits. I was only half a mile away, if that. Nothing.

And now I'm lying in bed in the dark, eyes wide open, thinking about it all. Going through it, like a film I've seen before. It feels unreal. The boy, I mean. Who was he? How did he and his dog know where I wanted to go? And the boy just seemed to vanish into the darkness, as if he wasn't actually there at all.

And then . . . *so did the dog*. I can't have imagined the dog, *surely*?

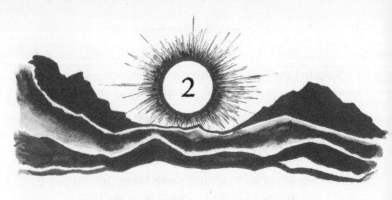

GHOST STORY

NEXT MORNING, WHEN I STUMBLE DOWNSTAIRS, Al Ramsden the farmer is on his knees with his head under the kitchen sink. He scrambles back out like a tortoise and nods at my dad. He's a big man, head sticking forward, eyelids drooping. Yes, definitely the tortoise type.

'That'll fix it. Shouldn't have no more trouble now, but if you do, you know where I live. It's no bother.'

'Thanks for that, Al.' Dad shakes his hand, grinning foolishly. He's obviously a bit embarrassed because he hasn't been able to mend the leaking pipe himself. 'Didn't bring any tools with me, that's the problem. Would you like a coffee? I'm just taking one out to Louise.'

'That'd be grand, as long as it's tea.' Al turns his head slowly and winks at me. 'So, you found your way back then?'

I realise that Mum and Dad must have gone over to the farm when they couldn't find me last night. I duck my head and concentrate on making myself a cup of hot chocolate.

'Eh, you're not the first. It's easy to get lost up there,' he says.

'Takes you by surprise if you're not watching out. You have to keep checking, all the time – you know, where the sun is, length of shadows, bits of broken wall or whatever.'

'Where that rabbit is . . .' Dad jokes. 'Oops, it's hopped away again!'

'I did get lost for a bit. But someone showed me the way.' I'm wondering if Al sent someone up from the farm to find me. 'I think it was a farm boy. He had a dog with him.'

'Farm boy?' Al screws up his face, thinking. 'There's no farm boys locally, only our Geoff, and he's a man of nearly thirty now with a farm of his own over Howshaw way. But there are two or three girls, on ours and the other farms. Fine lasses, fine helps. What did he look like?'

'I couldn't really see his face. He was about my age.'

Dad goes outside with a coffee for Mum, and I take my chance. 'And he had a dog called Bob.'

'Bob, eh? Are you sure of that?' Al takes a slow sip of his tea.

'Quite sure. He told the dog to take me home, and Bob brought me here.'

'Well, I can't rightly think who that might be.' The farmer pulls back a chair from the table and turns it round so he can sit astride it. He whistles a bit in a tuneless, thinking way. 'But others have seen a strange lad and his dog up there, over the years.'

'Over the years? What do you mean?'

'There's a story told round here . . . I'm not saying it's true. I've no idea whether it is or not. I'm not saying you'll want to hear it, neither.'

I can tell by the tone of his voice that he's going to tell me, whether I want to hear it or not, and actually, strangely, I do.

'Go on.' I sit opposite him at the table, nursing my cup of hot chocolate in my hands, and Al leans forward so his elbows are resting on his chair back. He closes his eyes. And he starts to tell me the story of a boy my age, who wandered over the moors with his dog.

Joseph and Bob.

And it's hundreds of years since they died.

*

Dad comes back in just as Al is getting into his tale and I'm listening in spite of myself. I'm a bit cold now. A bit cold with dread.

'They call him the Lost Lad.' Al is half-whispering, croaking his throat deliberately to make me nervous. 'And they say that Bob lived to a very old age, more than thirty years! And he can still be seen wandering the moors, following a young shepherd.'

'Do they now?' Dad laughs, and the spell is broken.

The farmer levers himself up. I'm breathing free again.

'Reckon I've put the wind up your boy here!' He chuckles. 'It's only a tale, Carl. Who knows whether it's true or not. But don't go moping about on the hills by yourself, now. It's easy for anyone to get lost, let alone a stranger, and you might not be so lucky next time. That's what the tale's about, I reckon.'

'Don't worry. We'll give the hills a miss today,' says Dad. 'I thought we'd drive over to Buxton for a change of scene.'

'Aye. See a few cars and shops!' Al agrees. 'Not that I go there meself very often. Don't like towns. But if you're ever stuck for summat to do, Carl, there's plenty going off at the farm right now. I can find you a bit of work for an hour or two, if you're bored.'

He and Dad walk out of the kitchen and I stare after them. Al's story has spooked me, that's for sure. What was he trying to tell me? That there are ghosts up there on the moor? A boy and a dog, just wandering? Year after year. Hundreds of years. It's rubbish.

'Take him home, Bob,' the boy had said. He definitely said that. But there must be loads of dogs called Bob.

But *home*. What did he mean, home? *My* home? But that's miles away. This cottage isn't *my* home. I've only been here a few days, yet his dog brought me here last night. How did he know where to bring me? *His* home? Is this, *was* this, his home? For a ridiculous, nightmarish moment I let myself believe the Lost Lad story. What if it's true? What if I've seen the ghost of a wandering shepherd boy?

Don't, Carl, I tell myself. Don't be stupid. It's only a story.

But I can't let it go. What if it *had* been him? What if he'd lived in this cottage with his family? Is my little room where he used to sleep? Had he sat in this kitchen, warmed himself by this fire, hung his coat on the hook on the back of the door, just like I do? Someone had done all of those things, of course they had, even if that very boy hadn't, even if Joseph the shepherd boy had never existed. The cottage is a few hundred years old. It used to be a farmhouse. Generations of families have lived here, been born here, spent their lives here. Eaten and slept and worked here. Laughed and sung and cried. And died here.

That's what people do. It makes me dizzy, thinking about it. Makes me scared.

But lots of things scare me now, since March 13th.

*

I tip the last of my hot chocolate down the sink, rinsing out the scum. Something makes me glance up. Out of the corner of my eye I can see something moving in the yard outside. I know it's my reflection in the kitchen window. It has to be. But I daren't look again. I've gone cold. My breath won't come right. I feel as if someone's watching me. I make myself look. There's nothing there. See, you idiot. Nothing. There's nothing to be scared of. Al probably made the whole thing up. It's like a fairy tale, warning kids not to go into the woods alone, scaring them with stories about wolves and witches. He was just trying to tell me not to get lost on the moors again.

'OK,' I say out loud. 'OK. Cool it.'

But if it wasn't a ghost on the moor last night, then who was it? I had definitely seen a boy of my age or a bit older. But Al had said there were no farm boys in the area. The boy must have been local though, or how would he have known where I was staying?

Did he really speak, or did I imagine it? Did he really say, 'take him home, Bob'? How did the dog know he meant here? The dog knew where to bring me . . .

Stop thinking. STOP IT. I'm going round in circles. Sometimes my brain does that these days. Sometimes it goes into such a tight spin that I can't stop it, can't get out of it, I have to crash, crash . . .

I shake my head, force myself to move about, clattering the breakfast dishes in the sink, making things normal. It doesn't matter who the boy was, not really. He helped me find my way home in the dark, that's all.

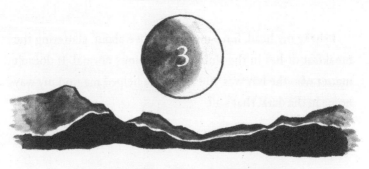

GIVE IT TIME

MUM DIDN'T WANT TO COME WITH US TO BUXTON. She was too involved in her photography. She's always the same when she's thinking about her photographs. People don't matter, it's just shapes and shadows and light that other people hardly even notice.

'No, I haven't got time today. Al told me it's going to rain tomorrow,' she says. 'Then I'll lose this golden early summer light. At the moment it's perfect for what I want.'

So we're going on our own, Dad and me. I feel a bit uncomfortable with him these days. He tries too hard to cheer me up. Mum seems to understand that I need my own silences, so she just prattles on in her own way without expecting a response from me. But Dad seems to be on a mission to bring me out of myself. As we drive, I do my best to respond to his jokes and his questions but I find it really tiring. He wears my brain out. I want to say, 'Leave me alone, Dad. It's OK.' He means well, I know. I've never known him to be quite so cheery with me, not since I was about five anyway, but I don't need that, don't want it. Sometimes, when I'm with other people, even Mum and Dad, I feel lost and on my own. I want to be inside myself, inside my head. I'm safer there, as if I've crawled into a dark cave where no one can reach me. I'm not so lonely there, with the walls keeping me from harm.

So anyway, on this trip out of the valley, Dad is behaving like a tour guide. He won't pass anything without remarking on it. Every so often he pulls the car into a lay-by and climbs out to admire the view, calling me to join him, pointing out small scars and rivers and plantations as if he's designed the landscape himself.

'I can't appreciate the scenery when I'm driving,' he says. 'It'll be great when you start to learn, in a few years. You can share the load a bit, take me out for a spin for a change.' And then he goes silent, probably wondering if he's said something that might upset me. Give up, Dad. I'm not made of china.

But he has upset me, actually. Suddenly I'm choked. I want to get out, I want to breathe. I can't talk to him now, can't think of another thing to say during the whole journey. I've crawled back again, into that black empty cave, and I don't know how I'll ever get out of it. We park the car in Buxton, and I just follow him around like an obedient dog as he looks at the old buildings and says how beautiful they are. He does his annoying best to grab my attention and share everything with me.

It shouldn't have happened, I keep thinking. *It was all my fault.*

Then Dad tows me through the park and along the river. We stop to listen to the ducks, and I think they're laughing as if someone's just told them a joke. I say that to Dad, and he just lifts his eyebrows. He sees a kingfisher streaking past, or he says he does. 'A blur of electric blue,' he mutters. 'Like magic, Carl.' He's really pleased; he loves this place. He wants me to love it too. And now I realise that we've stopped walking. We're sitting in a cafe, and I have no idea how we got here.

'What would you like?'

I stare at him, puzzled. I've been somewhere else.

'Carl, sometimes you look as if you've been dragged out of the ocean and you're still drowning.' Dad smiles at me sympathetically. 'Food? Look at the menu.'

I think I choose something. Maybe he chooses it for me. I eat it anyway. I look up again when I've finished, and Dad is watching me with a helpless expression on his face.

'What?'

'If you were old enough, I'd buy you a pint,' he says. 'You're lost, Carl. We don't know how to get to you, your mum and me.'

'It's not your fault.'

'It's not yours, either.'

'I wish he was here, that's all.' I push back my chair and turn my head away so I'm facing out of the window.

'We all do. We all miss him. We have to give it time, Carl. Things will get better, in time.'

Give it time. Give it time. Everyone says that. Aren't words easy to say? What the hell do they mean?

Dad sighs. He orders coffee for himself and asks me if I want ice cream. I shake my head. Little kids' treats. For ages we sit in silence. Elderly women gossip and munch around us, as waitresses bustle and smile. Dad takes out his phone to check his emails. 'Back in the real world,' he says. 'There's a good signal here.'

I don't bother. There's nobody I want to hear from.

He puts his phone away, and I'm getting his attention again.

'So, what was it you and Al Ramsden were talking about this morning?'

I shift uncomfortably in my seat. 'He was telling me about the Lost Lad. It's a kind of ghost story.'

Dad laughs. 'That man's a character, isn't he? A ghost story! A huge bloke like him, believing in ghosts!'

'He didn't say he believed it.'

'He's a good sort. Trying to buck you up, I'm sure. Telling you a fairy story!'

'I didn't say it was a fairy story. I said ghost story. Actually, I think it was a true story.' I'm getting annoyed with Dad now. He's always trying to be flippant, trying to make light of everything, treading on eggshells so he doesn't hurt me. Maybe I want to be hurt. Maybe I want to be broken.

'OK.' He drains his coffee and pushes the mug away, resigned. He stares at me, runs his hands through his hair, shakes his head. 'OK. Let's go home.'

'Home?'

'The cottage.'

I think he's given up on me, and I'm glad. He doesn't try to distract me with his idle remarks on the way back. I sag back in my seat and watch the green countryside flash past, observing nothing. When we're back at the farm track he stops the car and leaves the engine just idling, then he reaches over and puts his hand on my knee. I cringe away.

'That nice old theatre in Buxton reminded me of the time I took you and Jack to your first panto, when you were about six,' he says.

I flinch. *Jack.* We don't say his name out loud these days.

'You were into it right away. "He's behind you!" "Oh no, he isn't!" You were yelling yourself silly! And Jack, he was such a serious kid, wasn't he, when he was little? He kept looking at me as if to say, is it all right to laugh at this? Why is that man dressed as a woman? And when they asked for volunteers to come on stage, you were up there like a shot. And because you went, he followed. He was nearly in tears with nerves and worry, like a little lost waif, but he wouldn't let you go up there without him! And when you came back to your seats, he just couldn't stop giggling; he was so pleased with himself!' Dad chuckles, and I stare at him. 'You were both given a bag of sweets,' he goes on, still chuckling. 'And his had two lollipops in it and yours only had one! Remember? You were furious! You must remember!'

Am I supposed to laugh at this?

He starts to drive again, and the car bumps over the buckled stones of the yard. Dad waits for me to speak, and then he switches off the engine. 'Try to think about the good times, Carl.'

DARK SHAPE

WE HAVE TO STEP OVER THE FARM CAT TO GET through the porch, and she rolls on her back to snag us with her claws. Nasty Nellie, Al calls her. She seems to like to come to the cottage just to taunt us. She's actually the sort of cat I like best, because she's as ginger as a jar of marmalade and she's got a bit of spirit. I hesitate, stoop to stroke her, and she lashes out at me instantly. Gotcha! I pull a face at her, and she hisses.

Mum's in the cottage, sitting at her laptop. She looks up at us, smiling as we come in, flashes a concerned look at me and then gazes at her screen again.

'Had a good morning?' Dad asks. 'Lots of new photographs?'

'I'm just checking through them now,' Mum says. 'They're lovely. Yes, I'm pleased. This little cottage was so photogenic this morning! I'll do you a slide show, if you'd like to see them.'

We sit each side of her as the pictures slide across the screen; images of the cottage, the hills, the sheep, the fields, the trees, the usual stuff. I half watch, to please Mum, while Dad makes all the right noises about composition. The slide show goes full circle and pauses on the opening image of the cottage. It was taken from behind a tree that's in full leaf, so that the foreground, the branches, are slightly out of focus and shadowy, and the cottage is fully lit by the sun.

'That's the best one,' Mum says. 'I might frame a print of that for Al. What do you think, Carl? It would look lovely over the mantelpiece.'

I look at it properly. 'Who's that?' I ask.

'What do you mean?'

'That figure.' I point at the screen, at the dark shape under the tree.

Mum laughs. 'Nobody! It's just the way the shadows have fallen, where the soft focus is.'

Dad stands up so he's behind her, his hands resting on the back of her chair, and peers at the screen. 'I think I can see what Carl means,' he says. 'Can you zoom in to that bit?'

'It'll just make it fuzzier,' Mum says, clicking the zoom button. 'Look. It's just leaf shapes and branches, light and shadows.'

'You're right.' Dad leans forward and presses the key to zoom out of it. 'Funny, how the light can play tricks.'

I peer at it again. Well, they could be right. I move round to get a different perspective. Nothing is clear, and yet every time I look at it that little shadow of doubt comes into my mind. It *could* be a figure. It could be someone in dark clothes hiding among the trees, looking at our cottage.

It *is* someone. Watching.

*

I don't want to look at the photographs again. I lope up the winding stairs to my room. I have to tread in the middle of the steps, because hundreds of years of feet have worn them into a scoop. The bedroom door is so small that I have to duck to get under the lintel of the doorway, and again under a beam to get to the little low window. Someone has come into the room with me. I pause and turn back towards the door, thinking that Dad has followed me up here, but there's no one behind me. I've gone cold, damp with cold. The room has a strange feeling about it now, as if the bulging walls are breathing, leaning in towards me. It's as if they're *listening* to me. I have the sense that the beams of the ceiling are pressing down; as if the tiny windowpanes are eyes. My breath is beginning to flutter in my throat. I force myself to breathe deeply, steadily.

I can't get Al's story out of my mind. What if that shepherd boy Joseph really had lived here, all those years ago? Could this have been his room? But does it matter who it belonged to? Someone had to have slept in here before it was a holiday let, and before that, and before that, going back hundreds of years. Someone made these sloping floorboards creak as they walked across them, someone breathed on the window as they stooped to peer out of it. Just like me. I read somewhere that all rooms have ghosts. When I read it, I thought it was stupid. It *is* stupid.

I crouch down and sit on the deep, low windowsill, trying to think about what Dad said in the car. *Think about the good times.* To be honest, I can't actually remember anything at all about that pantomime he was on about. Maybe he made it up, just trying to make me smile. But he did get one thing right: when he was little, Jack was always the timid one. And then, something changed, and there was nothing I could do about it. Julius changed him. That's when I lost Jack.

And it was like losing part of myself.

TWIN FRIENDS

WE WERE BORN AT THE SAME TIME, ON THE same day, in the same hospital, and put in the same special care unit. That's how our mums first met and became best friends. They still are, they're like sisters. I've always called Jack's mum MumRuth, and he always called mine, MumLouise. Mum tells me that I wasn't actually born, I was lifted out of her by caesarean section (like a little Easter egg out of its wrapping, she says). It's enough to put you off chocolate for life. Jack nearly died before he was born because the umbilical cord was twisted around his neck. He only just made it. Both of us were really frail and had to be kept in incubators, and Mum says she and MumRuth shared a special time together, helping each other get through those long days and scary nights in hospital, and that's what made them so close. Mum never had any more children, but MumRuth had two more; Tamsin, just over a year younger than us, and then Anna. They're like annoying little sisters to me too. Well, Tamsin's all right now. They all have the same dreamy blue eyes and yellow hair, just a bit curly. Jack hated his curls as he grew older. He thought it made him look girly.

I try to picture him now, and I can't. Where's he gone? I start to panic. Don't slip away. Not yet. On our phones we have loads of photos of each other, grinning and gurning, mad selfies we've taken, a right pair of dudes. But I don't want to look at them. I haven't looked at my phone since March 13th.

Our mums have totally nothing else in common apart from the fact that they both ended up having special care on the day we were born. My mum is quick and busy and clever, and she can be a bit bossy sometimes. She likes to be in control of things. MumRuth is untidy and scatty. She's a lot of fun to be with. There isn't a dad there any more, but there are two grandads in the house. One's called Pops, and we all love him. The other's called Grandfather Henry. He's not much fun. They never have any money, that family. We have loads.

I'm brooding again. I can't go on like this. But I can't go downstairs. Not upset. That upsets them too; they tell me I've got to get better.

Think about the good times. Birthdays.

Actually, the last one was the best. January 2nd. Our thirteenth. We were teenagers at last! And it was snowing, just a bit – just enough to make it exciting.

I could hear Jack whooping like an owl as he came up the road, so I abandoned my breakfast and charged out of the house to meet him. He was riding a mountain bike, and he was grinning all over his face.

'You took your time, dude.' I couldn't take my eyes off his bike.

'Is that your present?'

'What did you get?'

'Nowt. I think they've forgotten.'

'Nah!' He wheeled the bike into the house to show Mum and Dad, and Mum gave him his present from them. It was a helmet, one with air vents and wheel adjusts so you can change the fitting with one hand while you're cycling. It was purple, like the bike. I felt just as excited as he did, but I wasn't about to show it.

'How cool is that!' he whistled.

I shrugged and sat down at the table to finish my toast, pretending everything was all right, then I saw Mum was laughing at me. 'Try the shed.'

Jack and I skidded round to the back garden and there it was, hopelessly disguised in newspaper, my own black mountain bike. I rode it round to the front of the house, yodelling like a goat, as Jack would say. MumRuth was just pulling up outside our house in her patchy old car. She wound down the window and handed me another roll of newspaper, like a bulky football, but I guessed what it was. It was my helmet from her. We stood our bikes side by side against the house, stroking them and admiring them, adjusting the seats heights, checking brakes and gears. We were totally in love with them, couldn't stop looking at them. I really don't know how his mum could have afforded to buy him one. She was a primary school teaching assistant, and there were six people in her house. I suppose my mum and dad might have helped her out a bit. They always call Jack, Numero Uno, because he was born first by about five minutes. Number One. They always treat him like another son. Did.

'Let's find a mountain,' I suggested.

'Be great,' he said. 'Only it's all flat around here.'

'Now we know,' I said.

'I've known it all along. It's always been flat.'

'No. Now we know why we're all going to the Derbyshire Peak District in the holidays. There's mountains there. At least two, Dad says. Loads of hills. Can't wait!'

'Park, then.'

'And on to the woods.'

We scorched off into the woods, sashaying round trees, ducking under branches, rearing over roots and stones, skidding, falling off, shouting at the tops of our voices like a couple of little kids. We had a hell of a time. It was a Saturday. We had all day to mess with our bikes.

'Are you twins or something?' the waitress at Pizza Hut asked, when we all met up later for our birthday tea. That's where we always go. Our bikes were chained next to each other just the other side of the window, where we could keep an eye on them. We were still a bit muddy, red-faced, slightly delirious and as hungry as lions.

I said yes, just for a laugh, and Jack said, 'Better than that. Best friends.'

It was a cool thing to say, that. Really cool.

YOU OWE ME A LIFE!

JACK SHOULD BE HERE NOW, IN THIS COTTAGE IN THE Derbyshire hills. He'd have loved it. We'd have brought our inflatable mattress for him, and he'd have his sleeping bag. He could just about have squeezed it into this little room, over in the corner where the roof ceiling slopes a bit. He'd have biffed his head every time he tried to sit up, but that wouldn't have mattered. We'd have talked all night. We'd have had our bikes propped up outside in the yard, and all the mountains and hills we could wish for.

He should have been here.

Think about the good times.

Our two families nearly always went on holiday together. The best time was in Cornwall, the summer before last. We'd just left primary school. Our family and Jack drove down in the big car with all the bedding and food and stuff, and the next day MumRuth, Tamsin and Anna came on the train. Their car was seriously old and wouldn't survive a long journey like that. We'd booked a cottage near Land's End, which is about as far away from home as you can get and still be in England. It feels like the end of the known world there. Dad calls it the Wild West. The car journey lasted nine hours, and for practically the whole of the drive Jack and I played games and watched YouTube on my iPad. Eventually, with miles of darkness behind us and ahead of us, we both fell asleep. When Mum shook us awake, we stumbled into the cottage like zombies and just rolled ourselves into our duvets without bothering to make up the beds.

'What's that noise?' Jack muttered, half inside his dream already. 'Like cars on the motorway . . .'

'It's the sea, dude.'

'Cool.'

Next morning Dad drove us to a cove called Porthcurno. He told us the name means port of Cornwall, but it was very tiny for a port, with such a narrow channel between the cliffs that I can only imagine fishing boats landing there. And the sea was the most amazing green, and as clear as ice. Mum was in her element. 'Just look at that colour!' she kept saying. 'Have you ever seen a colour like it? I don't even know a name for it.'

'Green,' Jack suggested.

'James Joyce called it snot-green,' Dad said. 'And he was a writer, so he should know. But maybe he was looking at it from a different place. Its colour is caused by phytoplankton in the water.' Being a teacher, Dad knows everything, and can't resist telling us. 'And the bed is all crushed shells of course. That's why the sand is so white. And, by the way, there are cables under the sea from here to Australia, America, just about everywhere in the world. Think of that! The original telegraph station is by the car park if you want to have a look . . .'

But Jack and I were already off exploring. The sea came in huge, striding glass walls that showered like crystal beads on to the beach. We ran in and out of the spray, screaming like six-year-olds, the waves clutching ice-cold manacles around our ankles. When we were soaked to the skin we flopped on to the shore and shook ourselves like wet dogs, shivering with cold. We found a stick and scrawled our names into the damp sand and watched the sea lick them clean away.

'That's you gone,' said Jack, dusting the sand off his fingers.

'Go, go, go!' I yelled, as fingers of water crawled into the letters of his name and finally wiped them away. 'Gone.'

Both gone.

Mum left us and drove off to Penzance to do some shopping and to visit a gallery. Later, she'd be picking up MumRuth and the girls from the train station. Dad went back with her to the car to fetch our swimming things, though it was a bit late as our clothes were already wet through. Instead of waiting for him we scrambled up the steep footpath that wound up and up to the top of the cliff and stopped there, gasping for breath, gazing down at the sheen of ice-green water below us. We could see a snorkeller in a wetsuit, nosing around the rocks like a big, black fish.

'He's pretending he's a whale,' Jack said. 'He might start really spouting in a minute!'

'I wonder if he can see those underwater cables Dad was on about.' I took a daring step forward to the cliff edge and leant out.

'Give up, they'll be well buried,' Jack said.

'Are you sure?' I leant further. Far below me the green sea glittered, clear as glass and speckled with white froth. Hardly anything grew on the cliff side; a few sprouts of fern and gorse clinging on the boulders, and then only the sea, churning and churning against the rocks at the very base, showering upwards like grasping fingers.

'Christ, watch it!'

I turned round quickly to look at Jack and lost my balance. I couldn't straighten up. I was teetering backwards. There was nothing behind me, nothing around me, nothing to grasp at but air. The weight of my body was pulling me backwards. I couldn't understand what was happening. I fought for my balance, swaying like a clown on a tightrope. Jack grabbed my T-shirt and hauled me back roughly towards him. It happened in a second. Then he threw me down on to the stony footpath, dashing the breath out of me.

'What did you do that for?' I was shouting.

'Maniac! You nearly went over then.'

'No, I didn't.' My heart was clamouring in my throat. 'I was totally fine. You pushed me. What the hell were you doing?'

'I was saving your life, you mutt.' He was half angry, half scared, laughing with no fun in his voice.

I struggled back on to my feet. 'If you say so.'

We went on for a bit along the cliff path but we'd lost our nerve, both of us. We were angry with each other, and scared and bewildered. I was beginning to shake uncontrollably. I pictured myself at the bottom of the cliff, being tossed backwards and forwards, crashing against the rocks, flopping in the water like a bundle of seaweed. I imagined Jack telling my parents, crying, all of them crying.

'Let's go back to the beach,' I said roughly. 'Dad might be looking for us.'

As we scrambled down the cliff path we could see Dad skidding his way down the steep sandy slope that led to the beach from the car park. He had our towels slung round his neck and he was swinging the bag of sandwiches that Mum had packed earlier. We ran to him, lolloping through the sand, safe now and warm again, both completely fine. We pulled on our swimming things and howled our way into the sea, then ran back to base, gritty sand sparkling on our legs. We sat with our towels round our shoulders eating the food, flapping greedy gulls away with our hands and feet, while Dad lay back with his baseball cap over his face and snoozed an hour away. We were hypnotised by the movement of the waves, trying to count the high ones, timing the crash as they sprawled out across the sand, trying to count the seconds between them.

'Every seventh wave is supposed to be big,' I said.

'That's rhubarb. They're all big.' Jack pointed to a black shape in the foam. 'What's that?'

'The snorkeller we saw earlier.'

'No. Something else.'

'It's a dog. It's drowning,' I said. We ditched our sandwiches and ran down to the surf's edge to get a clearer look.

'No way is that a dog. It's a seal, a cracking great seal!' Jack yelled. 'Eh, it's right nosy!'

The seal bobbed down away from sight and then came up again, closer, never taking its eyes off us.

'I wish it would come on the beach,' I said.

'We could wade out and swim with it!' Jack said. 'Imagine that, swimming with a seal, with a wild animal!'

'Cool!'

Jack took a deep breath 'It's fantastic here,' he said, gazing around him. 'I reckon this is the best day of my life.'

'Ever?'

'Ever. This is the best place I've ever been. I'm going to live here one day. I'll be a fisherman.'

'I thought you were going to be a famous TV chef.'

'That's another life. That's a spare one.'

'How come you can have two lives, dude?'

He sucked in his breath sharply. 'Because you owe me one, you haddock.'

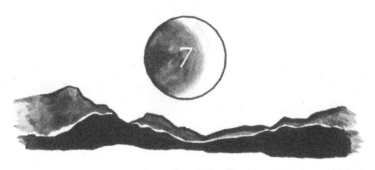

NO JACK

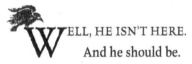ELL, HE ISN'T HERE.

And he should be.

He'd have liked it just as much as Cornwall. We'd have brought our bikes, we'd have raced them down that track to the farm and off up into the hills. We'd have been out all day, exploring and messing around.

But he isn't here.

I've had enough of this.

I slam downstairs again. Time has stood still down there in the kitchen, as if Mum and Dad have been frozen in some kind of spell. How long was I upstairs, thinking about our bikes and that day in Cornwall? Hours? Seconds? I've been somewhere else, and nothing down here has changed. Nasty Nellie is still glaring at me from the porch, stretching out her claws ready for a good scratch. Mum is still working on her laptop. Dad is still standing behind her, his hands on her shoulders, peering at another slide show of photographs and giving useless advice. He bends down and kisses the top of her head.

'Why did we have to come here?' I shout. I can't stop myself. There's no need to be angry with them, I know that. They look up, startled. 'We should never have come here, of all places. Don't you even care?'

Tears start up in Mum's eyes. She pushes back her chair, so it makes a cat-screech on the old stone slabs of the kitchen floor. 'Don't care! How can you say that?'

'Carl, this doesn't help,' Dad says.

'It does,' Mum mutters. 'Anger helps. It's natural. Let him be angry. Remember what Doctor Hassan said.'

'Don't psychoanalyse me!' I yell. I can hear my voice breaking as if it's in pain, and I don't care. I kick the table leg and it hurts my foot, and I don't care. I push a chair over and the leg snaps. I don't care about any of this. Dad has his hand on my shoulder, trying to soothe me. 'We should never have come,' I'm yelling. I can't control my voice. It's breaking up. 'Not now. Not here.'

Then Dad has me by the arms, trying to hold me or stop me, and I'm trying to fight him off. 'What would you have done if we'd stayed at home? We're here because Doctor Hassan advised us to take you away; for a change of scene, new things to do. What would you have done if we hadn't come?'

'Doctor Hassan, Doctor Hassan! What does he know? What does he know about anything?'

I'm nearly as strong as Dad is now. I push him away and he staggers back, falling against the side of the sink. I don't know whether I've hurt him or not. I don't care. I run outside and out of the yard. I run and run across Al Ramsden's fields until

I don't have breath to run any further. I throw myself on the ground and I bury my face in the grass and I let myself cry. I let the sobs heave out of me like the waves against the cliffs.

A WHITE FACE

NEXT MORNING IT'S AS IF NOTHING HAS HAPPENED. Mum's grumbling at Dad because he forgot to do the food shopping that she asked him to fetch while we were in Buxton. Dad just shrugs helplessly, making out he's the downtrodden male who always gets picked on, and I say nothing because I know the reason why he didn't do the shopping – because I was in such a downer of a mood, and I certainly wouldn't have relished trailing around Morrison's or Aldi after him.

'OK, OK, I'll do it now. There's a little shop in that garage on the main road,' Dad says. 'I can get most of the stuff we need there.'

'Let's all go,' Mum says brightly. 'It's about three miles, isn't it? It'll give us a decent walk before lunch.'

'I'd rather stay,' I say, and she gives me one of her worried, disappointed looks.

'No, you won't,' says Dad. 'I'm not leaving you here moping.'

'I'm not moping.'

'Feeling sad,' Mum says gently. 'Dad's right. What will you do, all on your own?'

I shrug. 'Al said I could help on the farm.'

'Would you like to do that?'

'Sounds cool.'

Mum frowns. 'I don't know. They're shifting sheep all over the place today. They'll be terribly busy. Don't get in the way.'

'I won't,' I say. Just go. Just go, I'm willing them. Just leave me on my own.

She cups my face in her hands and searches my eyes.

'I'm fine, Mum.'

She gives me a brief hug, and Dad just takes a deep breath as if he's out of his depth now.

I stand in the doorway and watch them striding down the lane together. Dad slips his hand into hers and she smiles up at him. They're lighter now, since yesterday, freer, and I feel the same. It's as if a thunderstorm has snapped and crashed and rumbled away into the distance.

I do mean to go to the farm, but first I want to look at Mum's photographs again. Something's niggling me about them. I switch on the computer and flick down the files till I find the ones we were looking at yesterday. She's already deleted a lot of them, but the one I'm looking for, the one of this cottage behind the hazy trees, is still there. At first glance it's simply a nice picture of a little cottage behind a tangle of foliage. What Mum calls a calendar picture. I can't see that shape I'd noticed yesterday. Maybe Mum has Photoshopped it to get rid of it. I'm just about to exit the folder and shut the computer down when I spot it again. That dark shape is so straight and thin that it could have been just another tree trunk. And yet it's different altogether, not tree-like at all, but human. Definitely. The more I look at it, the more clearly I see it. Surely there's an arm, a head slightly tilted, even a wisp of hair? And now I've found it, I can't not see it. Someone is hiding, lurking, watching the house. And the strangest thing of all is that Mum hadn't noticed, not even when she was taking the photograph. She doesn't just snap photographs, even with her phone camera. She's careful and slow, she thinks about it, she gets things just right. And yet she hadn't seen this person.

I move on to the next frame. It's a similar view but taken from a distance. I stare at it for a long time, examining it in sections. And then I see, clear as anything, the same shape; the same figure. Why didn't I see it before? I flick from one frame to the other and back again. I move on to the other photographs and find nothing, however hard I look, until I come to the final one of the day. Like the first two, it's a view of the cottage taken from behind the trees. It's a very arty shot, more typical of Mum's style, what she would call a 'Gothic composition of shadows and reflections' in one of her exhibition blurbs. She's focused on one of the downstairs windows of the cottage. The trees are now only seen by their reflection on the glass, so they look as if they're actually growing inside the house. It's quite disturbing, creepy almost. But creepiest of all is the pale glow, like a house light burning softly among the reflected trees.

But it isn't a lamp. It's a white face.

*

I shut down Mum's computer and kind of drift round the cottage, not sure what to do with myself now. It's weird, being in an empty house, especially when it's not home. There are all kinds of creaks and sighs going on, as if the place is alive and breathing, and in the end I'm so jittery that I go out into the yard. I go over to the clump of trees that are reflected in the window in Mum's photograph. They're clustered together, but when I wander through them I can see that there are one or two little spaces where someone could have stood, looking at the cottage. But why would someone lurk there like that? Why would they hide themselves in the trees?

And then I give a sudden laugh out loud. It was Mum! Of course it was! She'd have to stand there to get that angle right for the photograph, wouldn't she? It's her face that's reflected in the window; she was the stranger standing among the trees! How daft is that? Wait till I tell her!

I'm so chuffed and relieved when I realise this that I start off at a run for Al's farm. The sky looks in a bad mood and the hills are shrouded in a thin mist. All around me sheep are singing like our school choir – deep bellows like Reece and Bryn Jenkins and moans like the rest of us, and the high bleat of the lambs like the kids just up from primary school. It's a terrible racket. As I get closer to the farmyard, I can see the sheep all bumbling against each other. Al Ramsden is standing in the middle of them, shoving them into pens. He nods across to me and mouths something, but I can't hear anything above the row of the choir. Mrs Ramsden floats out of the farmhouse in her wispy, daydreaming way and wanders into the henhouse. She's a bit creepy, I think. I watch her kneeling in the straw to collect eggs, shifting the sitting hens so they squawk out of her way and flap outside, annoyed. I don't want to ask her for a job, not in the henhouse. I feel itchy just watching her.

A girl is heading a gang of rowdy sheep out of the yard and into a nearby field. She follows them through, lifting her arms and yipping, and a black and white collie darts round her feet. It's amazing to watch him, the way he crouches down and flattens himself almost to the ground, dodging towards any of the sheep that are trying to go the wrong way. Suddenly he has them all in his stare, and they rumble in a final rush into the field. The girl shuts the gate on them, and the dog bounds up to her, tongue lolling in that sloppy, adoring way dogs have. 'Well done, Moll,' she says.

Moll. Oh, not a boy dog then. A bitch, if it's OK to say that.

The girl's hair is flopping around her face, and she yanks a beanie out of her pocket and puts it on, stuffing her hair underneath it. And now I think about that boy on the moor top the other night; the boy who told his dog to take me home. Al had said there are no farm boys around here. Maybe it wasn't a boy at all. This girl is about the same height, she even walks like a farmer does, with long, steady strides. It could have been her all along. And the dog; black and white, or white and black, they all look the same to me, those farm dogs. Moll. Bob. It almost sounds the same. It *must* have been her. This is my day for solving mysteries. I lift my hand in a sort of 'Hi, remember me?' way, and she looks back at me blankly. I shove my hand in my pocket, feeling a bit foolish.

'Have you come to help us out?' Al shouts.

I shrug. 'If you like. I won't be much good, I shouldn't think.'

'You'll learn. We're bringing a few sheep down; you can give April a hand with that.'

The girl is still by the gate, and now there are two dogs winding around her feet. She waves her hand for me to follow and stomps off across the field with the dogs. I trail after her uselessly and without even turning she yells at me to shut the gate behind me. I make sure it clicks loudly so she can hear I've done it. The lambs are suddenly in a panic when they see the dogs coming, running to their mothers, bleating, butting their sides, and the mothers sniff them and let them get feeding. They're rounded into a jostling crowd of about fifty and then the girl and the dogs chivvy them off back down the field. Bossy-boots April tells me to open the gate for them and I run ahead, sending them scattering like kids in a playground. She whistles sharply and the dogs lie down, glaring at the sheep, who now trot through the gate obediently as if they're going on a school trip. I shut the gate behind them, breathless, and watch them being herded into the pen where Al is waiting.

'What's he going to do to them?' I ask.

April grins. 'If you must know, he's cleanin' the poo off their tails. It gets stuck, and he has to cut it off. Want to help?'

I shake my head, and she laughs.

'Want to drive the quad then?'

Now it's my turn to laugh. 'I can't drive! I'm too young!'

She shrugs. 'Suit yourself. I started when I was nine.' She swings herself on to the red quad bike and starts up the engine. 'Climb on,' she shouts. 'Sit on the edge of the trailer.'

So I do. Anything rather than just stand there with my

hands in my pockets like a useless townie. I perch behind her on the edge of the trailer, gripping it with both hands behind me in case I tumble off. The dogs leap on after me. We bump across the farmyard and when we reach the gate she yells at me to open it, and then waits for me to close it and climb back on again when she's driven through. I tense myself against the edge of the trailer. The sun is coming through the clouds now; the mist is lifting from the fell sides. It feels so good.

Sheep stream away from us. The ewes are bleating for their lambs to stay close; the lambs are hysterical because they can't find their mothers. The girl stops the quad and stands with her hands on her hips, watching them. 'They're all mucky. I'll tek them down to Al later,' she says. 'We'll do the ones in the top field first, and work back. I'm lookin' for cuckoos at the minute.'

'Cuckoos?' I say helplessly. I heard the cuckoo every day when we first came, in the trees, though it's changed its tune now. Why would a cuckoo hang about with a load of sheep? She steps forward and rummages round through the herd, feeling their sides.

'Just checkin',' she shouts. 'There's one or two haven't lambed yet. If we find any, we'll have to lump 'em into the trailer. We call late lambs cuckoos, that's what. Ever lifted a sheep?' I shake my head. 'It's like cartin' a great big sack of live potatoes.' Then she turns back to the quad and indicates the driver seat. 'Your go,' she says.

I hang back, confused.

'Get on.'

Is she bossy or what?

So I do. She leans across and turns the ignition key. 'Just flick that button on the handlebar,' she says. 'That's it. Slowly does it.' The bike edges forward, bumping and stuttering. I feel as if I don't know how to breathe any more. I'm clenching my jaw so hard that my teeth ache.

We judder across the field. When we reach the gate I'm yelling, 'How d'you stop it? Help! Help!' and she leans forward again and turns off the ignition. We jerk and buck to a halt. She runs to open the gate and waves me through, and I make it without scraping the sides, halting a bit more smoothly this time. Now I can breathe again. She yells at me to switch off and I climb down. I'm shaking, but I can't stop grinning. I look round to see if Al has noticed but he's bent over in the sheepfold, busy.

'Your turn,' I say. We go on, through three gates, swapping round each time we're through. In the fourth field, she's driving, kneeling on the seat, showing off I reckon, like a circus bareback rider. She stops the motor and jumps down.

'We'll tek some of this lot down to Al,' she says. 'I'll let the dogs tek 'em.' She whistles to the dogs to herd them down towards the gate and follows them herself. She doesn't climb back on to the quad.

'What will I do?' I yell after her, and she takes no notice, so I climb on to the quad and turn it on. I drive on my own slowly, slowly over the tussocky grass while sheep bustle around me, bleating and baaing. I steer carefully, terrified that I might run one of them over. I feel proud and strong, exhilarated. All around me are green fields and the golden fells, bright in sunshine now. I can hear the ripple of song from a bird, way up there, so high that I can't even see it. I'm alone with my thoughts again, and I feel good. For now, I feel alive.

Al is standing in the yard when I trundle back. He watches me as I park the quad by the lambing sheds. I'm feeling nervous again, clenching my jaw as though my teeth are stuck together with toffee, but I do it right, and he lifts a hand of approval.

'We'll make a farmer of you yet!' he calls. 'Come back any time.' He goes into one of the sheds, whistling. His wife ambles back into the farmhouse, not even acknowledging me. I don't think she's even noticed me. There's nothing left for me to do now but wander back to the cottage. The girl is whistling to the dogs, the sheep are rumbling around her. She's forgotten about me. She still hasn't said anything to show she recognises me from the other night, and so I say nothing about it either. I'd prefer to forget that I managed to get completely lost so close to the cottage. I still feel a bit dim about that.

As I trudge back, I realise that I've no idea who she is; Al's daughter, maybe, or just someone helping. April. Doesn't suit her, that name. November would be more appropriate.

*

'You did *what*?' Mum says later.

'It was only across the fields. I didn't go out on a lane or anything.'

'Did you enjoy it?' Dad asks.

'It was great!' I want to say, but don't. Instead, I just shrug. 'It was all right.'

Mum gives Dad a helpless look, but he just tucks his tongue in his cheek. I know that look well. It means, don't make a fuss.

Mum turns on her laptop. 'I'm doing a final edit on the photos I took yesterday,' she says. 'I want to narrow them down to half a dozen good ones. And I'm hoping I might get a chance to get some rainy ones later today. Look at the sky! Great black clouds rolling in, after all that sunshine. It changes every half hour! I love this place!'

'Run through them again,' says Dad. 'We'll give you the benefit of our humble opinion.'

I'm excited, remembering the discovery I'd made this morning. I don't want to blurt it out yet. See if they can work it out for themselves. They roll through the photos again. I stand quietly next to Dad, saying nothing. I'm feeling curiously nervous now. How weird. I make no comment when they come to the final one, the one with trees growing inside the cottage, with the white face at the window.

'I really like that one,' Dad says.

'I do too. Might be a bit too moody though,' says Mum.

I realise my breath is shaking. Neither of them has mentioned the reflected face, but surely they can see it. 'It's a bit spooky,' I say at last. 'That white blob.'

'It's a bit distracting, perhaps,' Dad agrees. 'Did you put a light on in the house?'

I take a chance. 'It looks like a face.'

Mum laughs. 'It looks like a white blob to me. It's not inside the cottage. It's just a reflection of the sun through the trees. I'll work on it.'

'Is it you, Mum? Taking the photograph? Your reflection?'

She looks at me as if I'm insane.

Of course it isn't. I take a last look at it, storing it in my memory to be nursed, and then turn away to the sink to get some water. I'm feeling faint with holding my breath for so long. So, if it isn't Mum's reflection, whose is it? With a start, I sense that there's something outside the window. I just catch a flicker of movement; it's as though somebody has been standing watching us and has quickly stepped away. I rush outside and run to the gate. I search all round, and then stand gazing up the lane that leads away to the farm. It's impossible for anyone to hide there. And yet. Surely. I did see something.

No. There's nobody there.

Dad joins me in the yard. 'You OK, Carl?'

'I thought there was someone there.'

'Where?'

'I'm not sure. Looking at us through the window.'

'I can't see anyone.'

'No.' I still feel puzzled. I can't let it go, and stay still, staring round me.

He touches my shoulder. 'It's all right. It doesn't matter. Come back in.' When he's like this, when he's gentle with me, it makes me feel weak and tearful. I know he's trying to help me. I know he thinks I'm imagining things all the time now. I know he wants me to feel better, but it makes me feel worse. I try to shake his hand off. I won't give way, not again.

'Tell me about that quad ride,' he says. 'You weren't on your own, I hope?'

'Not at first. There was a girl, showing me what to do.'

'Ah. A girl. Nice, was she?'

And he laughs, and I laugh with him. To please him.

'I met my first girlfriend when I was your age,' he goes on. 'Thirteen.'

'She's not . . . she's much older than me . . . it's not like that,' I mutter helplessly.

'Oh, so was this girl I'm talking about. I thought she was gorgeous. She never even looked at me. Not once. Didn't even know I was there! She was half a metre taller than me and looked right over my head!'

Funny. That's how Dad is – trying to make me laugh, trying to lighten things up. April's definitely not my girlfriend. I don't even like her. She's bossy and weird. But all that made me think about Jack again, and his sister Tamsin, who really is kind of pretty. That was something, I suppose. But then it made me think about Julius too. Julius Ferrero.

Hate him. Hate him. Hate him.

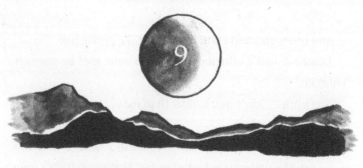

MERRYDAY CAFE

JACK AND I FIRST FOUND THE MERRYDAY CAFE JUST by chance, though I suppose it had been there for ages. We wandered up one of those side roads from the park, and we saw some older kids from our school going into the cafe. We thought that was a bit weird. Cafes were places we went to with Mum and Dad on holiday, not places for school kids.

'It's Ferrari's crowd,' Jack said, pulling a face. We'd only been at secondary school for a term and didn't know many of the older boys, but everyone knew Julius Ferrero. Everyone called him Ferrari. He was a real motorhead, apparently. There were prints of his car drawings all down the corridor outside the art room, all properly framed and that. Some liked him, some hated him, but you couldn't ignore him. Dad says that about Marmite.

'What they going in there for?' Jack said.

'To drink coffee, doh!'

'Must be rich then.'

'Ferrari? He is. Loads of money.'

'If I had loads of money, I wouldn't be spending it on cups of coffee!'

We scrunched our noses against the glass, trying to see what they were ordering. 'Doughnuts!' I guessed, sighing. Jack stood back a bit, puffing out his cheeks. I thought he was making faces at his own reflection in the glass. Then he let out a long, slow whistle. I tried to see what he was staring at. A waitress was coming towards Julius's table. She was wearing a black dress with a low top, and she had really black shiny hair and huge, dark eyes.

'She's beautiful!' Jack whispered.

'Yes,' I agreed.

She wasn't beautiful like my mum, when she's sleepy and smiley and warm, or like Tamsin, with her yellow curly hair and her bluebell eyes, or even like glossy-lip Miss Dolby from last year in primary school. The waitress was just film-star gorgeous. She must have known we were watching her because she glanced up and smiled. I went scarlet and I bet Jack did too.

Ferrari was idly dealing out cards on to the tabletop, as if he'd never even noticed her. Card playing was a massive craze in the upper school. I didn't get it. What a waste of time.

Jack punched me softly on the arm. 'Hey, what!' he said.

'Hey, what?'

He blew the waitress a kiss, giggling, and so did I. This time she flapped her hand at us, as if we were annoying flies to be shooed away, and we jerked our heads back, embarrassed suddenly. Ferrari raised his head for a moment and gave us an amused smile, then he said something to the other kids, and they all looked at us, laughing.

'Get lost, Ferrari,' I muttered. I shoved my fists in my pockets and walked away. 'See you, Jack,' I shouted over my shoulder. 'I've got better things to do.'

'So've I,' he said. I didn't slow down, but he caught up with me.

'Come to ours,' he said. 'We can finish that new plane.'

'What's it like to have a girlfriend?' I wondered, just casual, just kind of shrugging to show I knew it was a daft question.

'Like eating doughnuts every day.'

We scrambled off to his and forgot about the waitress. Anyway, she was old. Probably about twenty.

Jack's two grandpas were in the kitchen, as usual, waiting for their tea. They didn't get on at all. They were about as alike as a stick of rhubarb and an apple tree. Grandfather Henry was all bony fingers and gloomy eyes. Pops, MumRuth's father, was loose and untidy like the rest of the family, with white fizzy dandelion-fluff hair and smiley eyes. On the wall over the chair where he always sat there was a cartoon that he'd drawn of himself as a teenager. It was in black and white except for a pair of bright red boxing gloves. It was really funny. He said it was a caricature of a photo of himself on the day he joined the army, before they made him cut his hair and smarten himself up. I couldn't imagine him as a soldier. He was much too easy-going, as if nothing mattered, ever – nothing worried him. He was always in the way and wanting to help, dropping plates or burning things.

'Oh, crikey, I've spilt it again!' he was saying as we went in, and we grinned at each other. What's new? MumRuth steered him to his chair opposite Grandfather Henry and told him she'd be quicker without his help, thanks. Everyone loved Pops.

Grandfather Henry, though, was as grumpy as an old dog – never liked his food, never seemed to like anything much. MumRuth didn't have to look after him, he wasn't even her dad, and his son, her husband, had disappeared years ago with 'another woman'. But she's like that, MumRuth, she's just kind, she can't help it.

We had to climb over Grandfather Henry's legs to get to the stairs. He always sat with his feet stretched out in front of him, and when we tried to pass him, he lifted up one of his legs like a gate. He always did that. Never said anything. Grandpa Pops chuckled and rubbed his hands together as if it was all a great joke. 'Where are you two off to?'

'Airfix planes.'

'Oh, crikey, I love them. Want any help?'

'No thanks.'

'How're you getting on with the new ones?'

'Cool.'

'Just give me a shout.'

We always stored our planes in Jack's bedroom, not mine. They hung from the beams like swarming bats, drifting slightly when you opened the door or the skylight. Pops had bought our latest models for us last week. Jack's was a red triplane kit, and mine was a model Avro 504.

'These are First World War planes,' he told us when he gave them to us. 'Beautiful things, they are. Jacko, you can be the Red Baron. And Carl here can be Edward Mannock. And I want you to find out who they were on that computer thing.'

'Why, don't you know?' Jack asked, acting innocent.

'Course I do. I know everything.'

We were just doing the last bit of putting the stickers on when we heard Pops lumbering up the stairs after us. Jack pulled a face at me.

'Who were they then?' Pops wasn't even in the room before he was asking us.

'The Red Baron was Baron von something,' Jack said, trying to remember and glaring at me to help him. I knew the word, but I couldn't pronounce it.

'Baron von Richthofen.' Pops lowered himself on to Jack's bed with a grunt, and held out his freckled hand to hold the plane. 'And? What do you know about him?'

'He was Germany's top flying ace in the First World War.'

'Aye, lad. You got it right. What about your man, Carl?'

'Edward Mannock. He was England's top flying ace.'

'Let's get the stickers on then. Finish the job.'

He fumbled to do it with his big, bumpy fingers, breathing heavily, almost snoring with concentration. 'Just look at them! Beautiful, like dragonflies!'

He handed them to us. We held them up in the air, zooming them towards each other, making deep roaring sounds in the backs of our throats.

'You vill die, you Enklish dok! Take zat!'

'Cripes! You've taken my gunner! You swine!'

Pops held up his hands as if he was trying to catch the planes if they fell. 'Imagine those pilots sitting in them, high up in the sky! Flimsy bits of gossamer, that's all they were. Bicycles with wings. Imagine the pilots up there having dogfights in open cockpits, guns blazing all around. They were sitting targets.'

We were ignoring Pops, arms high, making our planes loop the loop, veer round each other, gunning, swooping, roaring, while he chuntered on.

'Imagine how brave they were. And when they were shot down, they fell to the ground. They weren't allowed parachutes. They just fell like dead birds out of the sky.'

His voice was shaking then. I saw that his hands were trembling. I stopped. Mannock's plane paused in mid-air. I'd never seen Pops like this before. 'Oh, War isn't a game, boys. It's for real.' He took out his handkerchief and blew into it, long and loud, like a blaring trumpet. 'I know about war. My big brother was in the second one. He was killed. It's not a game. I want you to know that. It's not a game.'

We were embarrassed then. We didn't know what to say to Pops to make him stop crying. Jack was daring me with his eyes not to laugh out loud. He was squirming and red-faced, he was embarrassed. I turned my back on him. I didn't know what to say to either of them, so I went downstairs, climbed over Grandfather Henry's leg, and went home past the Merryday Cafe. I didn't even bother to see if the beautiful waitress was still there.

10

GIRLS

EVERY TIME WE WENT PAST MERRYDAY CAFE WE glanced in to giggle at Julius and his card-playing friends. Some of them were girls, ignored by the boys. I felt sorry for them, but they didn't seem to mind. They just seemed to want to be seen hanging round with Julius. It was weird. Every so often he would favour one of them with a slow smile, but it was never the same one. If the girls saw us watching they used to narrow their eyes at us and mouth 'Clear off, little brats' or something. And we did, shrugging. We lost interest in the cafe after a bit, or pretended we did.

Then one day Jack texted me: *It's time we got it over with.*

I knew exactly what he was talking about but decided to ignore it.

'What do you think?' he asked me on the way to school the next day. We were wobbling about on our old bikes. We'd had them since we were ten, so they were far too small for us, but it was quicker than walking.

'About what?'

'You know. Girls and that.' He giggled a bit.

I said that most girls were rubbish but Tamsin was all right, and I darted him a look to see how he'd taken it. He said nothing, just screwed up his face as if he was eating lemons.

'What's got you?'

'Everyone says that,' he muttered.

'Well, she is. Don't you think so?'

'How would I know? I'm her brother. It's incest to fancy your sister.'

'I didn't say I fancy her. I said she was all right.'

Jack began to ride away. 'Just don't mess with her, that's all,' he shouted over his shoulder.

'What's that supposed to mean?'

'You know. Asking her out. Just don't.'

I watched him as he rode off; Jack-in-a-huff. He liked to be that way sometimes. I didn't care. I wondered then what it must be like to have a sister – a real sister. MumRuth and my mum always said we were one big family; in a way it was true. We did nearly everything together. When Tamsin was little and before Anna was born the three of us used to play together, usually in our garden. Theirs was just a backyard really, and a pretty messy one at that, with knee-high grass and weeds and faded plastic toys lost in it. Actually, I liked it better than ours, with its flowery borders and neat lawn that Dad sweated over when he was mowing. Tamsin moaned if Jack and I wanted to go somewhere else and she had to stay behind, and very often we'd just give up or take her with us. When she first started at primary school in Reception and we were in Year One, I used to look after her in the playground when Jack wasn't there. I'd fight anyone who pushed her around, which was more than Jack would do. I often called her Sis, as a joke, but that didn't actually make her my sister. Anyway, it was none of his business whether I liked her or not. But why on earth would I want to mess with her, or anyone else? He was the one who wanted to have a girlfriend, not me.

Jack was showing off as he rode away, trying to make that rusty old bike of his buck like a horse. He nearly crashed into a bin lorry parked in the road.

'You're rubbish!' I shouted.

He didn't laugh. Didn't even turn round.

I hated that. It's not true that I didn't care when he went off in a huff. I hated it when he was mad with me, but I had to find a way of getting a girlfriend first. That'll show him, I thought.

So, I asked a girl out. I didn't really mean to, not on that particular day. Eva, her name was. She had silky hair that swung and bounced when she walked. She wore it in a tight ponytail when she was in school but as soon as she came out, she untwisted the band that was holding it in place and let her hair tumble loose around her shoulders, like yellow water. I liked that. When Jack wasn't around, I liked to follow her out of the playground, just to watch how her hair rippled. She must have noticed, because one afternoon she glanced round at me and smiled, and I just said it.

'Fancy coming down to the park?'

I've no idea how I managed to blurt that out. My heart was hammering, and my mouth was dry and itchy as if there were shreds of feathers inside it. Suddenly I'd no idea whether to put my hands in my pockets or fold my arms or tuck them behind my back. I'd never even thought about hands before. The instant I said it I regretted it, miserable because I knew she would just laugh at me, but she gave me that shy smile of hers and said, 'I don't mind,' and ran her fingers through that river of hair, and I didn't regret it after all. We walked on to the park, hardly saying anything. I coughed a few times to get rid of the feathers, and she giggled a bit.

We went straight to the little kids' roundabout. Eva sat on the bar and I ran round the outside, pushing it, hoping I wouldn't stumble and make a fool of myself. I felt silly, so I put one foot on the board and hopped along as if I was pushing a scooter, but I still felt daft, even though she wasn't watching me but was staring straight ahead, as if the roundabout was some sort of driverless bus and she was going home on it. I did notice that she was gripping the bar with both hands. Eventually I got tired of scooting and jumped on board. We were freewheeling then, the roundabout spinning on its own axle and the green park swinging round us. She let go of the bar and stood up unsteadily, laughing, her hair wisping behind her. I laughed back. 'I like you. I like you,' I chanted under my breath. When the roundabout slowed down, we did the whole thing all over again, and again, until for some reason we were both laughing helplessly.

'Stop now,' she said suddenly. I jumped off to slow it down so she could step off. She picked up her school bag and slung it over her shoulder. 'Got to go.'

'Shall we come again tomorrow?' I asked, dizzy.

'I don't mind.' She tucked her head down as if she wasn't even speaking to me. 'There's someone watching us,' she muttered, and hurried away.

I swung round, and just caught sight of Jack loping off in the other direction. 'Jack!' I shouted, but he pretended not to hear me. I ran home by a different path, looping round some shrubs so I didn't overtake Eva. I didn't want her to think I was following her. I didn't want to follow Jack either, so I took a bit of a zigzag route to keep myself away from them both and still on course for home. I was mad with Jack. Why hadn't he waited for me? What was he doing there anyway? Surely, he wasn't spying on us? I couldn't understand why he'd been there watching us instead of being stuck in front of a computer game at home. In a way I was half pleased that he'd seen me with Eva, but that didn't excuse him. He'd probably scared her off. She'd left so suddenly, just cut me off, when we'd been having a great time. It was all his fault. Finally, out of breath, I sat on a bench and messaged him. *What were you doing, spying on me?*

He messaged back. *It's my park too.*

Eva and I went to the park again the next day, and this time she was much more talkative, in fact I would say she was a bit of a motormouth. I was used to that. My mother talks too much, except when she's concentrating on her work. I'm used to letting the words flow over me. It was just a trickle of nonsense that has nothing to do with my own thoughts. Maybe Eva was nervous. She seemed to know everything that needed to be known about the Strictly show on TV, which I'd never seen and wasn't interested in, so I just zoned out and enjoyed the walk, being with her, passing kids from our school and grinning at them. Her arm was swinging so close to mine that I could have touched her hand if I'd dared. Her hair swung in gleaming waterfall strands as she walked. I wanted to stroke it. We stopped by the duck pond and sat on the bench that was dedicated to someone who 'loved this place'. Little kids were crouching on the bank, chucking bread into the water, their grown-ups clutching the hoods of their jackets so they didn't fall in. Ducks streamed towards them, cackling with greed. Their ducklings bobbed behind them like little wind-up toys.

'They're like jewels, them. What d'you call them?' Eva asked.

'Mallards.' I was proud that I knew the answer.

'They're pretty.'

So are you, I thought, but didn't dare say it.

'I like the way they make that kind of V-shape with their paddling,' I said instead. 'Like corrugated water.'

Eva stared at them, combing her hair with her fingers.

'I like your hair too,' I muttered. My voice went a little bit out of control, and she giggled. Embarrassed, I jumped up and ran to the mossy stones around the far end of the pond as if I was trying to get a better look at the ducks. She sauntered after me and stepped on to one of the stones, so I did too. We both tried to walk on them. They were more slippery than I expected, so I had to concentrate hard not to fall in. I jumped off on to the safety of the footpath, but Eva spread out her arms like a trapeze walker and stayed on, perfectly still, then lifted a knee up so she was poised amazingly on one leg. She turned her head to smile proudly at me, and then her expression changed, as if she was distracted by something behind me. Then she started to wobble. I leapt forward to grab her hand. And so did Jack. He just seemed to appear out of nowhere, a genie out of a lamp; he must have been hiding, watching us all that time. He reached her first and pulled her to safety, and it was just like that time on the cliff in Cornwall, though it was obvious by now that she'd regained her balance and didn't need any help at all. She glared at Jack, furious with him. He stepped away, hands behind his back, grinning foolishly.

'What are you doing here?' Eva demanded.

'Just happened to be passing.' He raised his eyebrows at me and turned away, paused as if he expected me to follow him, and then shrugged and walked off.

Eva scowled at me. 'I'm going.'

I'd wanted to tell her how good she looked on the stones. I'd wanted to walk her home, make plans for tomorrow, hold her hand this time to show her I liked her. She didn't give me a chance.

'Don't bother seeing me again. You're all right, but I don't like your freaky friend.' She flounced off, Eva of the bouncing hair.

And I let her go.

I ran to catch up with Jack. I didn't know what to think any more. Maybe I should have punched him. We walked fast, saying nothing, looking nowhere. At the end of his street, we stopped to catch breath.

'What was all that about?' I panted.

'We're all right, aren't we?' he said.

'I suppose so.'

'Girls get in the way.'

Two weeks later, I saw him with Monika Lenski, another girl in our year. I was gutted to see them together. I saw them by chance, at least I think it was by chance, when I was in town on Saturday morning getting some bike oil. I certainly hadn't been following them. I didn't even know they were seeing each other. He pretended he hadn't seen me at first, in fact I thought he was just going to ignore me. Then he caught her hand in his and grinned at me. It wasn't a proper grin, he just kind of bared his teeth. I turned to look in a shop window, biting my lip. He brought her straight up to me and stopped, so all three of us were looking at a display of carpet cleaners.

'Doing anything tonight?' he asked.

I shook my head, not trusting myself to speak.

'D'you want to come over later?'

'There's a crowd,' I mumbled.

'You mean, *three's* a crowd,' Monika said. I hated her bright, clever laugh. I hated her, I hated him.

I didn't hear from him for a few days, didn't speak to him at school, didn't actually see him around because I wasn't looking for him. I spent time with Reece and Bryn, who really *are* twins and so alike that everybody gets them mixed up. I think Reece is slightly fatter. They asked me no questions, just let me hang round with them. I began to feel I liked their company best anyway. I supposed Jack was going round with Monika, and I certainly didn't want to see them together. But I knew she'd dumped him when I met him loitering by the school gates one afternoon, obviously waiting for me. No cheery grin, no punch on the arm, he just fell in step with me and loped along beside me, head down. He's like a dog that's been kicked, I thought. Serve him right.

'She wasn't right for you,' I said.

He shrugged.

I stopped and held up my hand, palm out, and we slapped hands solemnly.

After that it was just us again, the way things had always been. Just us.

I still fancied Tamsin, though I didn't talk about her again. She's all right. She's a good laugh. Everyone says she's stunning, actually. She looks like Jack. That's the uncanny thing, because when I try to remember what Jack looks like, I can't, but when I try to think of Tamsin, up she comes, full of smiles and good fun.

I'M GONNA LIVE
FOR EVER!

'COMING ROUND THE WOODS TONIGHT?' JACK texted me later, and I stopped the game I was on and cycled over to his straight away. It was a way of making it up, I knew, after the Eva and Monika Lenski business. Best ride for weeks, that was, even though our bikes were old and knackered. We nearly killed ourselves whizzing under trees, and then we parked up by the biggest, like we always did, and started to climb it. It was our challenge, every ride.

'I wonder what kind of tree it is?' I asked. I was reaching up as far as I could, my knees gripping the trunk so hard they hurt. This time, I thought, I'm really going to get to the top.

'Sweet chestnut.' Jack's voice came from somewhere above my head in the foliage. I slid down again and looked for a better angle.

'How do you know?'

'Reception class, Mrs Whatsername with the wobbly voice?

Telling us about chestnut tree candles? And collecting leaves in autumn term to decorate the classroom? Don't you remember chestnuts and conkers and sycamore wings? Ash keys? Acorns? Don't you keep anything in that empty skull of yours?' He did it in Mrs Whatsername's wobbly voice while he was shinning up the tree, finding footholds that now were perfectly obvious, gripping the arms of branches as he swung across. I hoisted myself up again by leaning my bike against the trunk and standing on the saddle, and then the bike skittered away from me and left me dangling from a branch. He easily reached the highest branch before I was halfway up.

'I'm gonna live for ever!' he sang, taunting me. 'I'm gonna live for ever!'

'Oh no, you're not!' I snarled at him, annoyed because I couldn't remember the names of trees from infant school and he could, and sick because he was a better climber than I was. I caught hold of his leg and tried to pull him off, and he slid down to my branch, yodelling like a maniac. He was holding one arm up, and when he was next to me he showed me what he had cupped in his hand. It was an egg.

'You shouldn't do that,' I said. I was really shocked. It just wasn't the sort of thing Jack would do, usually. Ever. 'The mother might desert the nest.'

'You shouldn't have pulled me down. I was going to put it back.'

'You shouldn't even have touched it. She'd have smelt you on it. Your stink!'

Jack held the egg out on the flat of his palm. It rolled off and tumbled through the branches below us. 'Oops!' he said.

'You did that on purpose.'

'Who cares? It was probably only a crow. Who cares about crows? Carl? Carl?' That was in his favourite croaky voice, which he always did when he wanted to annoy me.

I tried to push him off the branch, I was so angry with him then. He scrambled down the tree like an ape, swinging from branch to branch by his arms and legs, and then hung from the lowest one upside down, his knees wrapped around it. The contents of his pockets trickled down to the ground – a few coins, his bus pass, a pencil torch. A packet of cigarettes.

I felt as if he'd grown up and left me behind. I felt ill. I wormed my way down the tree and pulled him off the branch, and I started pummelling him, tried to get his face into the tiny mess of eggshell and its mucus. We rolled over and over down the bumpy slope of roots and fallen branches. We were both panting for breath. We meant it. We meant to hurt each other. A passing cyclist swerved to avoid us. 'Oi! Pack it in!' We both sat up, gasping. Jack wiped his nose on the back of his wrist and held out his hand to me.

'Shake,' he said.

'Yuck! I don't want your snot!' I rolled away and picked up the packet of cigarettes. 'What d'you need these for, ape-head?'

'What d'you think, cloth-brain?' Then he grinned sheepishly. 'I found them after my dad left home. I thought, I'll keep these to remember him by.'

'But you were only about seven when he left. You've kept them for five whole years!'

For some insane reason, we both thought this was hilarious.

We shoved the cigarettes one by one into a leaf pile till they stood in a row like little white soldiers, and then we stamped on them, every one. We laughed till we were croaking like a pair of raggedy old crows.

THAT GIRL APRIL

I'M WALKING OVER TO AL'S FARM WITH MUM WHEN I see that girl again. She overtakes us with her long farmer's strides, and I say hello to her. She has earphones in, and I don't think she hears me. She doesn't seem to notice me. I feel stupid, shove my hands into my pockets, cough a bit as if I hadn't really said anything.

'Who's that?' Mum asks.

'I think she's called April. She was at the farm the other day when I was there.'

'Is she the one who taught you to ride the quad?'

I grin, in spite of myself. 'It was good that. Good fun.'

Mum smiles back. 'I'm glad. Just be—'

'Careful. OK.'

When we reach the farmhouse, Al is sweeping Nasty Nellie out of the kitchen with a stiff yard brush. His wife watches, hands fluttering awkwardly as she tries to do the same sweeping motion in the air. Is she weird or something? The cat spits and lashes at them both with its evil claws.

'Don't know why we bother with this one,' Al says. 'All she does is scratch us. Don't let her in if she comes your way.'

'She already has,' Mum says. 'She yowls at the door like a little lost ghost.'

'Don't feed her. Let her scream. She's supposed to catch mice. She's useless.'

'We've come to see if you can find another job for this bored boy,' Mum says.

I look at her. Bored? Who says I am?

'Aye, I can that. He can come and do a bit of walling with me. Fancy that, Carl?'

I shrug, and foolishly bend down to stroke the cat. Her claws rip my hand. Mrs Ramsden cackles softly and tiptoes away.

Al rummages through the wellies in the porch. 'Find a pair that fit you. Ideally you should be in boots. Don't want to go dropping stones on your toes. Take a pair of them thick gloves too.'

We walk side by side along the track to one of the top fields. Al's chuntering to himself as if he's lining up his jobs for the day. I can hear April rounding up sheep with her dog, whistling and yipping. Al pauses for a moment, letting the sound in. 'Fine shepherd, that lass. I can trust her with my sheep any day.'

'Is she your daughter?'

'As good as. Actually, I don't know whose lass she is, and that's the truth. She tells us nowt. Why, fancy her, do you?'

'No!' I say quickly. Is that all grown-ups think about?

'Aye, she's a bit old for you!' He laughs. 'Mind you, everyone looks about fifteen to me these days. That's what happens when you're my age.'

'Where does she live?'

'Not sure. Over the knoll somewhere, I think. Can never get her to say owt about her family.' He jerks his head towards the gloomy fell where I lost myself that other night. So that's it. She has to walk right over there to go to her own farm. It was definitely that girl who showed me the way back home. I knew it was.

'She stays here though,' Al went on. 'Beds down on the settee in front of the fire, stays a few weeks and then moves on. She comes and goes as she pleases, that one. Always has done. But I can always find summat for her to do. She turned up one April, when the lambing had just started. Been coming four years or so, always about that time. Did the same this year, couple of months back. So that's what we call her. April.' He stops and looks back towards the farmhouse. 'Actually, my wife gave her that name. Always wanted a daughter. Lost one, eighteen years back. Broke her up. Aye, she fancied the name April back then. No idea what her real name is, but it fits, and she doesn't seem to mind.'

My head is buzzing now. I'm trying to figure out what it must be like to be that girl, coming and going like a stranger, answering to a name that doesn't belong to her. But I'm thinking about something else too, that night I got lost. I'm trying again to fit her into the image of that figure who came out of the darkness.

'There's a proper bedroom always here,' Al's saying. 'Waiting for her, if she ever asks for it. We've never told her. We don't want to scare her away. It's up to her.'

I'm hardly listening to him. I break into his words. 'But

maybe she walked home, over the knoll I mean, the other night, about four days ago? Maybe it wasn't a boy I saw, it was her.' For some reason I'm starting to shake now; my lungs are tight. I'm willing him to agree with me. It must have been her. Not a ghost boy at all. It really matters. I need to believe that there isn't a ghost boy haunting the moors, haunting our cottage, haunting my room, my dreams. Can't he see that it really matters? But Al says nothing at all. Completely ignores me, or is deaf, or busy thinking about his farm or the daughter he lost all those years ago.

We've reached a stretch of tumbled-down wall, and he drops down on to his haunches. There's stones scattered across the grass, as if someone's given the wall a big push.

'You see what it's like? This is the bane of a farmer's life, I can tell you,' he says. 'Town folk get themselves lost and just climb over the nearest wall. Promise me you'll never do that. There's paths and signposts and stiles all over the place, and yet they have to climb the walls and the gates instead of looking for the proper way out of a field, and someone like me has to go mending the walls back or else lose his stock.'

'I wouldn't do it,' I say.

'Aye. Mebbe. This is a day's work now, just this stretch. It takes an experienced eye to pick out the right stone for the right place, and I'll not ask you to do that because it'll take you a fortnight else. You can help me move all these stones away, and then I'm going to take it all back down to the foundation. I do a good job; it's always worth it. There's something beautiful about a well-made drystone wall, I always think. See how it's made? Go on, you tell me.'

He stands back with his hands on his hips, watching me as I study the sound part of the wall. 'Well, the big stones are at the top,' I say.

'They're the coping stones. And . . .'

'It's deeper at the bottom than it is at the top. Thicker. And the stones get smaller till they get to the . . . the coping stones.' Coping stones. What a strange idea. People are always saying to Jack's mum, 'How are you coping?'

'And . . .'

I bite my lip, scanning the sound stretch of the wall. I want to get it right, to prove to Al that I'm not just a gormless townie, getting lost and wandering where I shouldn't be, climbing over walls and gates. 'Every now and then there's a flat stone sticking right through!' I feel proud of myself.

'Aye. Them's called through stones. And what are they for?'

'Stepping on, to climb over?'

'Tcha!' he says, annoyed.

I've let him down there, I can see.

'Get sorting them into piles. Big stones there, through stones there, smaller ones there. And the little ones we'll use for packing, just like bits of rubble.'

I watch his big hands sorting out the boulders and fitting them into place on the wall, as if he's doing a jigsaw. I have a feeling that he doesn't really need me to help him at all, but I do what he asks me to, and we both work in silence. The stones are much heavier than they look. I grunt when I try to lift up a particularly heavy flat stone, and Al swings it easily out of my clutch and fits it neatly across the shelf of stones below it. 'A through stone is to strengthen the wall,' he mutters. 'Not for climbing on. Now you know, don't forget it.' And then, still without looking at me, still bending, lifting, swinging, placing in his easy, thoughtful rhythm, he says, 'I used to do this kind of thing with Pete, from the neighbouring farm. He was my best pal. I lost him a couple of years back.'

So, this is what it's all about. Probably Dad has asked him to have a word with me, about *coping*. How does an old man like Al know what it feels like?

He looks at me then, to see if I want to say anything, and I don't.

Al chuckles. 'Now my mate Pete, he was a bit overweight. Liked his beer a bit. No harm done. Cracking good farmer. He had this stick, hazel it was, knobbly, with a bent bit like an elbow. He loved that stick. And when he died, his wife Mary said, "What would you like to remember him by?" And I said, "That stick, Mary. That bit of tree." I keep it in the kitchen, leaning against the corner.'

'I've seen it.'

'Nice to have something. Nobody thinks about what it's like to lose your best pal. That's why I wanted it, that old stick. Something that always reminds me of him. Keeps him alive in my mind, I suppose.'

He straightens up, and we're both listening into the silence – only there isn't a silence; there's a breeze ruffling the long grass, there's the sound of the river and, high up, the endless, endless churning of that bird again.

'Grand, isn't it?' Al says. 'Know what bird it is, Carl?'

I shake my head.

'It's a lark. Skylark. She sings her heart out till it could burst, that little one, up she goes, rising, rising. Just listen to that.'

SKYLARK

AND WHEN HE SAYS THAT, I'M LOST AGAIN. I'M remembering a particular day last October when I went round to Jack's after school. Their kitchen smelt of bacon and beans. MumRuth indicated with her head that Jack was up in his room, and I picked my way through the junk that was their family: doll's house furniture, fairy wings, roller skates, books, magazines, shoes . . . and wandered upstairs into silence. Jack was sitting cross-legged on the floor wearing headphones, eyes closed. I tapped his shoulder. He kept his eyes closed. 'Shh!'

I sat and waited, impatient, drumming my fingers on my knee. I wanted us to play a game on my iPad. Outside, kids were playing, shrieking, in their backyards. Buses trundled past, shaking the house. At last, he took off his headphones and opened his eyes, but he was still far away, somewhere so deep inside himself that he looked as if he didn't even recognise me.

'What is it?' I asked.

He shook his head. 'You wouldn't get it.'

'Try me.'

He unplugged his earphones from the machine and put the music back on, loud. It was on a CD, so it must have been around the house a bit. It wasn't the sort of band stuff we usually listen to. It was more the sort of thing Mum and Dad listen to at home. It was a violin playing a fluttering, butterfly sort of tune that dipped and rose and sank and rose again. It made me feel quite tingly and uncomfortable. It seemed to go on for ever. Jack didn't move until the last note had been played. It was so high-pitched, it set my teeth on edge. You wouldn't believe an instrument could make such a high sound. When it died away, the room sort of jangled with the memory of it. I didn't dare speak till Jack did.

'Pops gave it to me.' He handed me the old CD cover. 'It's about a lark,' he said. 'It's called "The Lark Ascending". It's by Vaughan Williams.' He pronounced it Vorgan, and that made me smile a bit, because even I knew you pronounced it Vorn. 'Don't you dare say you don't like it, or I'll kill you.'

'I do like it.' It was all right, I suppose. Kind of beautiful, in a weird way. It scared me a bit because it was so, I don't know, passionate I suppose, emotional, but I didn't say that. Jack gets these fixes about things. He probably listened to that music about a hundred times. He even started whistling it, in an annoying, flutey kind of way between his teeth that I'd noticed other kids in school doing, trying to sound like that nut-case Ferrari. I couldn't do it. But I got to know that tune as well as Jack did. Weird, isn't it, that you can hear a tune even when it's not there? How does that happen? But when he was whistling, I always knew it was because something was on his mind. That's how he was.

So, he was walking next to me one day, whistling it, and I knew something was coming. 'Have you got shopping to do?' he asked me casually. I quite often had to shop on the way home if Mum was involved in one of her projects and Dad had meetings or whatever after school. I nodded. 'Pizzas and stuff.'

'I'll come with you,' he said. 'I just want to show you something on the way.' He led me to the Barnardo's charity shop on the high street. As we went in, the woman behind the counter looked up from her Kindle and smiled fondly at him, as if he was her favourite nephew.

'Hello, love. Back again?' Her cheeks were the dark purple of tuna fish, I noticed.

'It might be the last time,' he said mysteriously, and the shop woman actually winked at him.

Jack threaded his way past the stands of cardigans and old ladies' dresses to the back of the shop, where there were shelves of books, CDs, DVDs, mismatching crockery and badly framed watercolours. A box of soft toys spilt out across the floor, and he absent-mindedly kicked aside a forlorn teddy and stopped in front of a black fabric violin case.

'Twenty pounds,' he said softly. 'What d'you think of that?'

'I think it's a fiddle case,' I said, bewildered. What on earth was going on? My eyes were straying towards a pair of red boxing gloves. They reminded me suddenly of that cartoon that Pops had drawn of himself. I wondered vaguely whether they were my size. Jack nudged me, and I looked at the violin case again. 'Do you get anything with it?'

The shop woman brought her heavy scent of chemical roses

towards us and lifted down the case. She took it to the counter and unzipped and clicked it open, revealing a highly varnished violin snug inside it.

'Gorgeous, isn't it!' she sighed. She stroked the red velvet lining of the case. 'I once had a dress like this. I cried when it didn't fit me any more. That's the trouble with growing up.'

She lifted out the violin and handed it to Jack, and then unclipped the bow that was tucked inside the lid. 'Go on, love, give us a tune on it.'

Jack plucked the strings with his nails as if he was playing a guitar. 'I've got ten pounds of my own,' he muttered to me. 'In my pocket, right now. How much have you got?'

'A tenner,' I said. 'But—'

'Can you lend it me?'

'I told you, I'm supposed to be getting myself a pizza. Mum and Dad are both out.'

'I can make you one at home.'

The woman was looking from one to the other of us, eyebrows raised, tuna cheeks bunched in a smile. 'Ah,' she said. 'What a nice friend.'

So, I handed over my ten-pound note. The shopkeeper looked as pleased as Jack did. Her cheeks flushed a deeper purple, her eyes seemed to mist over. It was obvious that Jack had been haunting her charity shop for days, weeks probably, ogling and stroking that fiddle. She watched every move he made as he gently put it back into its case and zipped it up, then showed him how the strap worked so he could sling it over his shoulder like a professional – casual, proud. He was grinning as if his face was lit by sunshine.

'Come back and play me a tune on it one day.'

'I will,' he promised. 'I'll play you a waltz so you can dance round the shop with Carl.'

I squirmed.

'This is amazing!' he kept saying as we walked to his place. 'I've got it! I've got it!'

'Now all you have to do is to learn how to play it,' I reminded him.

'No problem.'

'Do you even know how to tune it?'

'No idea! But I'm going to join the school orchestra.'

I nearly choked. 'Never! You're never bringing it to school! You're walking in on your own, mate.'

But he did it. The Julius Ferrero gang bayed like a pack of hounds when they saw him. Nothing escapes their mockery. Ferrari himself, I noticed, just watched Jack, cool as ice, his eyes narrowed, his lips twisted in a strange smile that wasn't exactly mocking, surprisingly. It might even be said to be approving, though it was hard to tell with a character like him. Jack even braved the Brunton brothers, who just shouted animal-like 'Yahs!' and false roars of mocking laughter. But they let him pass. They would certainly have bashed my nose and probably the fiddle too if I'd been carrying it. But Jack walked straight through the middle of them as if he didn't even know they were there. Perhaps he didn't. Perhaps he was so intent on his violin and the skylark music that was soaring through his head that he actually wasn't aware of anything else at all. But I followed warily, watchful for him; my fists were clenched in my pockets and my stomach quaking inside and out. I thought about those red boxing gloves dangling uselessly in the charity shop. I might need them.

He went straight to the music room. I loitered outside, listening to the awful strangled-cat noises of the violin being tuned up. Eventually he came out without it, but still smiling.

It was safe to be seen with him now, so I walked with him to registration. 'So? Is she going to let you join the orchestra?'

'I've got to learn to play it first, like you said. Have lessons, like.'

'Oh.' My heart went out to him. One lesson probably cost as much as the fiddle itself. There was no way his mum could afford it, I knew that. 'P'raps you could do it online,' I suggested, and his eyes brightened.

'She said she'd set it up for me, whatever that means. She's got to change the bridge or something. She's going to show me what the strings stand for, like what notes they're supposed to make. She says they're a bit tired, and it needs new ones. But they cost ever so much. Good ones are more than the violin cost!' His eyes were round with the importance of it all. 'She might sneak me a set from the school supplies, only I mustn't tell anyone.'

'Right,' I said, and grinned. 'Thanks for telling me! And what does she think of the fiddle?' Somehow, I couldn't bring myself to call it a violin. That meant classical music, proper stuff, far beyond the likes of Jack.

'She didn't exactly say I've got a bargain. It's made in China, and those outfits only cost about sixty pound new, she said. She said it's fine for a beginner, it's got a good tone, she said! And I could have paid hundreds, thousands, for a different make. For the bow alone! So we did all right, Carl, didn't we?'

We? So I'm in this too. And I realised what it meant. He gets these fixes about things, always has done, and we both do them for months – like the model planes, or this and that craze. But fiddle? He'd be doing that on his own. I'd just have to sit and listen to him practising, that's what he meant.

A NIGHT OF CROWS

I BREAK INTO THAT BIRDSONG; I'VE HAD ENOUGH OF it. I want to talk about something else now. Al bends down again to heave up his stones, his hands cradling them as if they're precious. Something's ringing in my head that I want to ask him about, and then I remember what it is.

'That story,' I say. 'The one you were telling me the other day.' He looks at me, disappointed. He was wanting to tell me more about his dead friend Pete, and I don't want to hear any of it. 'You know, that story about the boy who wanders around the moors.'

'Aye. The boy with the dog. The Lost Lad.'

'Is it true, Al?'

'How do I know? It's a story. That's all. A bit of truth here, a bit of nonsense there.' He puts his hand to his eyes and looks across through the sunlight to the roof of a distant farm. 'See that place? That's where my pal lived. Pete, who I was telling you about. It's good to see it there, his old home. It's good to think about him from time to time. Come on,' he says abruptly.

'We've done here, Carl.'

He strides ahead of me down to his farm, his arms swinging, his big hands shedding their working gloves like thick dusty skins. We're finished, the conversation is over. He's done what he promised Mum and Dad he'd do. I see it now. He wanted to talk about his friend Pete, that's all. It's a conspiracy between him and my parents, this game of finding things for me to do at the farm. He doesn't need my help. He'd be able to get on much faster without me. That wall probably didn't need mending at all.

I pull back, letting him go. I turn round again to look at the wall and I see a man, an old man with white hair, leaning against it. He's a big man with a twisted walking stick. I see that the stick has a bent elbow and I know the man is Al's friend Pete. But he's dead, long dead. Crows are pecking at him. I can't get away fast enough.

*

'Was it good?' Mum asks when I get home. She's putting food on the table, freshly bought from the service station shop; bread, cheeses, slices of ham, a jar of onions bobbing in brown vinegar, blood-red tomatoes. 'Wash your hands,' she orders. 'Eat.'

I can't talk. Something's going wrong in my head again, the way it does, and I can't stop it. It's as if bluebottles are buzzing inside it; it's like fizz. Black thoughts are bobbing through it like tadpoles. Not tadpoles. Black feathers, floating. I realise I'm stuffing the food down my throat and Dad's coughing politely to tell me that he'd quite like some too and Mum's beaming as if the whole scene is a photograph that she's just created. 'I knew some hard manual labour would do you good,' she says. 'You'll sleep well tonight.'

But I don't. I go to my room, and there's that silence there, that breathing silence, and when I get into bed and close my eyes, it's as if the whole house is listening to it, waiting for something. There's a creaking and a shuffling. I'm convinced somebody else is there, in that room with me. I can't get away from it. I can't shut it out.

Now they come, and I know what it is. It's almost as if I've been waiting for it to happen. Crows. Carl! Carl! Carl! I can't get away from the sound of crows. It's happened before; several times since March 13th. It's like a recurring nightmare, only I'm wide awake and I can't stop it. I can hear them circling like doom birds, like a Kansas tornado, a twister, round and round the cottage, round and round the trees. I can hear the flap and slap of their wings, and the creak of their cries. 'Carl, Carl,' they go. I cover my head with a pillow, I throw it off, I sit up. They're tapping at the window with their beaks; they're scrabbling at the sill outside.

'Go away!' I shout, feeble, useless. I can hardly hear my own voice for the din they're making. The croaking stops. Now I hear a strange thudding sound, I see black shapes dropping past my window, I see them on the ground, wings spread, still. Black litter.

I run downstairs, tripping on the slippery steps, and I leap the last few.

'What's up?' Dad calls from their bedroom. The cottage lights come on as he stumbles after me.

'There's birds dropping out of the sky,' I yell. I wrench open the door and run out, hunching my shoulders against the drop of bird bodies. Dad is running after me.

'Where?'

I'm expecting to see bird carcasses everywhere; I'm expecting to tread on them. But there's nothing. Nothing. I stare blankly.

'I did hear them,' I say. 'I saw them falling.'

Dad points to a black feather, pinned slantwise into the ground like an arrow. He pulls it out and I take it from him.

'But there were hundreds of them. I heard them.'

He takes me into the cottage and I sit at the kitchen table with the feather in my hand, strumming the hairs. Dad's making hot chocolate and toast for us both. He hums around the kitchen, looking like a deckchair in his striped multi-coloured dressing gown. He riddles the fire to make it flare up again, chucks a log on to it. It's all normal and cheerful. Mum comes down, sleepy, yawning, sits next to me with her head resting on my shoulder. She takes the feather from me.

'It's rather lovely,' she says. 'Look at the beautiful blue sheen on it. It's a flight feather, this. You can tell by the way the hairs are long on one side and short on the other. How fine the hairs are, look, towards the quill end of the shaft. You could make a pen out of this, probably.'

I think I'm feeling better. It's cosy. It's like being a little child again, being comforted after a bad dream. I realise how kind Mum and Dad are, not minding that I've woken them up in the middle of the night. They're doing so much for me, they really care. Dad's even taken time off school for my sake, to bring me here. We were only supposed to come for a few days and we're still here. Why are we staying? To help me get better. Why? *Am I ill?* I sip my hot chocolate. The butter on the toast melts and drips down my fingers, and I lick them clean.

*

The next morning, I'm sitting just by the gate of our cottage and that farm girl April strolls in. She looks surprised to see me sitting there, as if she'd expected to find the place empty. She doesn't explain why she's come into the cottage garden, just squats down next to me. I'm still trilling the hairs of that feather, and she takes it out of my hands. It's almost as if that's what she's come for.

'Crow or rook?'

I shrug. 'I don't know the difference. Is there one?'

'If there's more than one crow, they're rooks. If there's only one rook, it's a crow.'

'There were hundreds of them. I heard them in the night.'

'They're a right menace,' she says. She sticks the feather in her hair. 'Vampires. They steal eggs. Ma Ramsden hates them. Haven't you ever heard of a murder of crows? They're cunnin' killers. You see them stickin' their greedy beaks inside holes in trees and pullin' out eggs and chicks. Baby squirrels sometimes. They eat lambs' eyes. They're murderers. But there's ways of gettin' rid of them.'

'Shooting them, you mean.'

'If it's allowed. Stonin' them. Stone the crows – you never heard that?'

I nod. I even smile in my head, picturing Al's jittery wife with a catapult aiming into the trees.

'They're a damn nuisance, they are. All farmers hate them.'

She stands up and aims the feather perfectly so it lands shaft down, arrowed into the earth like it was last night.

I stare at it. 'Mum thinks they're beautiful.'

'Aye, they're that too,' she agrees. 'Sheeny shiny. They sometimes leave gifts behind. Glittery things. Eh, and me, I love the sound they make.' She stands with her legs apart, seems to draw herself up, thrusts her neck forwards. She cocks her head from side to side, spying the feather from one eye, then the next. Then she steps forward, awkward, jerky, feet wide apart. I can't take my eyes off her, fascinated. I don't know whether she's wanting to make me laugh or what. She has me. She stretches her arms behind her, slopes her shoulders, then thrusts out a rasping caw! Her whole body jerks with the sound. Again and again, and again, and each caw! caw! caw! is wrenching her body. I back off, scared. She's a crow. She's a crow. At last, she stops, exhausted. She's a girl again, grinning.

Yes, she scared me, all right.

'What's up?' she says, as if she doesn't know. 'Don't you like birds?'

THAT WHISTLE

I USED TO. WE SOMETIMES USED TO GO BIRD-watching, me and Jack. It was one of his crazes, one of the many. We were always collecting something, and it was usually his idea, and he wouldn't talk about anything else till we did it together. When we were three or four, it was plastic dinosaurs. We knew the names of them by heart and used to recite them solemnly every day. I can still do it now, if I think about it. Tyrannosaurus. Spinosaurus. Brachiosaurus. Apatosaurus. Pterodactyl . . . My mum can do it with prayers and poetry she learnt at school. MumRuth said dinosaurs gave her a headache, but Pops loved them as much as we did. He used to lower himself down on to his hands and knees and show us how to make caves for them out of empty boxes. 'Bring us a bit of jungle,' he would say, and send us out into the garden for pieces of fern and twigs, and we would do dinosaur roars till we were hoarse, all three of us.

Die-cast model cars came next. We loved their polished bright colours, tiny steering wheels, the opening bonnets and boots and doors, just like the real thing. Best of all were the friction models that you had to strop several times before you set them free to streak across the floor and crash into chair legs. Jack's favourite model was a fire engine with an articulated ladder. It spent every night on his pillow. Mine was a white Lamborghini Aventador. Pops taught me how to say the name and it rolled on my tongue like a lollipop. I kept that in my pocket. I loved it. We used to line all the vehicles up in order of style, make, colour, size, number of doors, newness, favourites – any combination. Classic cars, service vehicles. Eventually we stopped playing with them, just like that. They queued up along the skirting board of Jack's room, like a silent traffic jam. Maybe they're still there, gathering dust and fluff.

But I wish I'd never set eyes on that white Lamborghini.

After the die-cast cars, it was knights that we collected, Lego, superhero stickers, bugs. We were about eight then. I was usually the one with enough saved-up birthday money to buy them, but we always played with them at his house. Mum liked to have everything tidied away before I went to bed. It was never as good if we couldn't litter the floor with them and find them there in exactly the same place the next day. When we were nine, it was jokes. *What did the hat say to the scarf?* I don't know, what did the hat say to the scarf? *You go on ahead while I hang around.* We got that from Pops. Dad says everybody loves a joker. I'm not so sure, Dad. Not all the time.

Then late last year, when we were really into computer games and nothing else, Mum said we needed to go out and get some fresh air, so that was when we turned into bird-watchers.

We used Dad's binoculars and Mum's bird books, and we used to get up early to creep through the woods. At first, we couldn't see any birds at all, but we could hear them all right, busy with their twittering and rustling, and sometimes a clatter of alarm and then scary silence. We'd finally trudge back to his place for breakfast, famished.

'I don't get it,' Jack grumbled. 'There must be some birds somewhere. Why won't they show themselves?'

'Perhaps you were making too much noise,' MumRuth suggested. We looked at each other.

'It was you!' I said to Jack. 'You go in there stomping about like an elephant in football boots.'

'That's it,' said Pops. 'You must learn to creep like a fox. Listen. And lurk.' He did a demonstration, tiptoeing round the kitchen, finger to his lips. Grandfather Henry stretched out his leg to try and trip him up.

We liked bird-watching because we loved going into the woods so much. It was our place, the place we went to without grown-ups, especially when it was getting dusk. It was really echoey in wintertime, when the trees were bare. We used to try to scare each other sometimes, for a laugh, yelling out suddenly when everything went really still, like it does sometimes when all the birds have suddenly gone quiet. 'Caw!' one of us would yell, and make the other one jump out of his skin. Jack was the best at playing tricks.

So, there was this time when we were going home one sleety afternoon in January. We'd been out on our new bikes, trying to spot golden eagles or something daft, and I got a puncture.

I was pushing my bike and Jack was wobbling in half circles on his so he could keep at my walking speed. He was whistling in that new, flutey sort of way that he'd picked up from Ferrari at school, and it irritated me because I didn't like Ferrari, and also because I couldn't do it. It wasn't long before half the school was trying to do it, strolling like Ferrari, chirruping away like overgrown budgies. I must admit I tried to copy it myself, when I was in the loo or some other private place, but I couldn't find the rise and fall of it, couldn't do a tune with it, so when Jack picked it up just like that and added a sort of music to it, it made me sick. He had that tune too, that skylark tune; he could do every bit of it in the Ferrari whistle.

'How d'you do that?' I didn't want him to think I'd had several goes at it and failed. I didn't actually want him to think that I liked it at all, because I didn't. I hated it. 'You sound like a parrot,' I added, giggling.

'You have to be the seventh son of a seventh son,' Jack said mysteriously. 'Actually, Ferrari taught it me.'

I knew that already of course, but I wouldn't let on. 'Ferrari!' I said scornfully. 'What do you want to hang about with him for?'

Jack shrugged. 'I don't. I just like the way he whistles, that's all.'

I went silent. Jack trilled on.

Ferrari and his followers were three years ahead of us. He had to be *the* most arrogant boy in the school. He had the richest parents, and the soppy good looks of a boy-band singer; even I could see that. And he was a real motorhead. That's why everyone called him Ferrari instead of his real name. Ferrari is the make of a super-sleek Italian car that people pay stupid money for. Most kids reckoned he was very clever; some said he was the cleverest boy in the school, not like the dopes who hung around with him who were thick as tree trunks. That's being unkind to tree trunks, probably. And they were right bullies. Ferrari never joined in with the bullying. But he never stopped them either. He just watched, lounging against a wall. Whistling.

What he actually did to people was worse. He would just stroll across to someone and mention something embarrassing about them and keep repeating it till he reduced them to tears. He tried it on me for a bit when I was in Year Seven, about my eczema. I wouldn't cry. I wouldn't even hear him. It hurt, all the same.

He did something else which was even worse than that, if you can imagine it. Sometimes he would decide he liked you. If he chose you, for an hour or a day or a few weeks, whatever suited him, he'd make a point of waiting for you; in the corridor, at the gates, anywhere. He'd fall in beside you, tell you nice things about yourself, sling his arm casually across your shoulder, offer you chewing gum or peppermints or cigarettes. At first it was flattering, because he made you feel special, and then it was embarrassing because you knew everyone was watching; and then it made you anxious and insecure, and just when you got to the point where you couldn't do without Julius, when you needed him to be there, when you looked out for him all the time, he'd drop you. You'd see him shadowing somebody else, being matey. Boy or girl, Year Seven or any year. 'Hi, Julius,' you'd say. He'd ignore you. As far as he was concerned, you no longer existed.

That was Ferrari. I hated him. I hate him more than ever now. I'll never forgive him for what he did to Jack.

Anyway, maybe I just upset Jack for going on about his whistling. He didn't sound anything like a parrot! We stopped near that tree, the climbing tree where he'd dropped the egg that time. I leant my bike against the trunk and stopped for a pee, and when I turned round, he'd gone. He must have lifted up his bike and crept away, and I hadn't heard a thing.

I looked round nearby bushes and shrubs, thinking he was hiding, but there was no sign of him. 'Come on, I give up!' I shouted, slightly miffed. It wasn't funny any more. All I got back was silence. 'OK. I'm going without you. I'm bored,' I said. I started to push my bike through the scrub, listening out for him all the time, watching out for any flicker of movement. I shouted again, and still my voice fell into silence. An owl shrieked near my head, and I yelled with fright. The moon had risen, the shadows were grey. The sides of the trees were streaked with silver, turning them into ghosts. Twigs snapped under my feet, the undergrowth around me rustled as if there were people there, lurking, watching. I hurried on, holding my breath. I wanted to leave my bike behind and run, it was such an awkward thing to be pushing.

I really thought I was lost. Nothing seemed familiar any more. All the branches leant out to scratch my face, roots tripped up my feet, twigs snagged my clothes. But at last, I was free, back in civilisation. There was grass under my feet, there were street lamps in the distance. Cars were droning again. And I could see Jack sitting on a bench, flicking through his mobile. He didn't look up till I reached him again, then he glanced at me casually and grinned. 'You took your time.'

'I was enjoying it. It was good in there without you trilling away. Owls and stuff.'

'Great.'

We walked along in silence, both pushing our bikes, and then I leant towards him and screeched in his ear, just like the owl.

THE CRASHED CAR

IF I'M THINKING ABOUT BIRDS, I HAVE TO THINK about the day of the crashed car.

It looked as if it had swerved off the main track through the woods and gone headlong into a tree. The bonnet was buckled up like a crumpled paper bag, and the driver's door was open but listing awkwardly sideways, like a broken wing. We ran towards it instinctively, and then stopped. Jack put his hand on my arm. 'What if the driver's still inside it?'

'I know. He might be dead or something.'

'We ought to tell someone.'

'We ought to look.'

We were scared then, scared of what we might find. We crept closer to it, and my heart was thudding. The car stank of hot metal. There was an eerie kind of frightened silence around it, as if even the birds had scarpered from the scene.

'It might explode,' Jack said.

We backed away, uncertain what to do next. We didn't want to just leave it; we didn't want to go any nearer. Then I saw someone sitting hunched up a few metres away from the car, his back against a tree. He had his head in his hands and he was moaning softly. It was a boy, a bit older than us.

'He's hurt,' Jack whispered.

'But he's OK. He's alive.'

'Can't be the driver though. He looks too young.'

We moved forward again, still nervous. What if there were bodies in the car?

'Are you all right?' I called, nervous.

The boy looked up briefly, and we knew him. He covered his face again. We could see that his hands were red with blood. He muttered something and staggered to his feet and lurched away from us, doubled up and stumbling, and we hadn't the wit to follow him. We let him go, because we knew who he was and we didn't want to know. It was Ferrari. He didn't want us to see him, and like fools, we pretended we hadn't. We said nothing to each other either. We just stood looking in silence at the wrecked car, and at last I went up to it and looked inside. It was empty. I knew it would be.

Jack came then and stood next to me, whistling softly to himself.

'So he was driving it.' His voice was shaking.

'What should we do?' I asked him.

'Nothing,' he said.

Nothing is what we did.

Nothing is so easy.

We just stood there till the silence stopped, till the rooks or the crows or whatever were croaking again, and we turned and ran off home.

I should have phoned the police. I should have talked to Mum and Dad about it. If I had, the nightmare that was March 13th would never have happened.

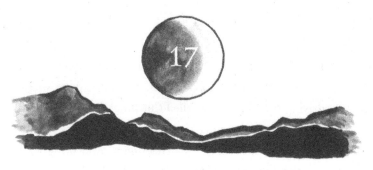

THE VOICE IN
THE ROCKS

FANCY COMING FOR A WALK WITH US?' MUM SAYS, coming into the yard.

I start, shake myself out of some kind of trance I'm in and realise she's talking to April, who just grins and shakes her head. 'Got stuff to do,' she mutters, drops the crow feather at my feet and walks off.

'She's a nice girl,' Mum says, watching her.

'She's weird.' I crouch down, pick up the feather and try to snap it. It just bends and springs back into shape.

'Oh, I thought you were friends.' Mum smiles. She gives me the sort of look that's saying, 'you need friends; it'll be good for you to have someone to talk to', then she changes her mind. She's said it all before. 'I've packed some sandwiches for us,' she says cheerily. 'We're all going for a drive and then I thought we could walk along Derwent Edge, up above Ladybower Reservoir. There's some amazing sandstone rocks up there, Al told me.

All strange shapes moulded by the wind. I'd love to see them.'

Dad's packing the car with rucksacks and camera gear. 'You'll need your walking boots, Carl,' he calls. 'Guess where we're driving to? It's a place called Cutthroat Bridge. Who on earth thought up a name like that?' He chuckles. They're both being cheery. It's deafening, this cheeriness. 'And bring your waterproofs. I don't like the look of those clouds.'

'Why are we going then, if it's going to rain?' I ask.

'I'm not,' he says. 'I'm going to drop Mum there and meet up later. I want to go to a museum near the reservoir. It's all about the dam busters. Did you know they practised on that reservoir?'

I shrug. He's being a teacher again.

'You can walk the Edge with Mum, or come to the museum with me.'

'Great.'

'You have heard of the dam busters? The great heroes of the Second World War?'

'Course,' I lie.

'Well, come on then. It's history. It's exciting stuff. Planes, Carl. You're mad about planes.'

'That was ages ago, Dad. Don't you remember? I don't want to think about them any more.'

I decide to go with Mum. I tell myself that standing around every five minutes while she composes her photographs in the rain is marginally better than two hours of Dad's lectures. Mum's pleased, I can tell. I don't spend much time with her usually. It's strange being alone with my parents so much. They irritate me quite a lot these days. Sometimes I even wish I was back at school. But there's a kind of comforting order to their lives too; they do things in a certain way – preparing a meal, preparing to go out, preparing for bed. Their day is laid out before them and they only have to follow the mapping. That's what it looks like, anyway. They always seem to know what they're going to do next. So, Dad drops us off at Cutthroat Bridge and waves cheerily, and Mum waves cheerily back at him, and I dig my hands in my pockets and trudge after her.

It's a long hike up from the bridge, and pretty boring going across the grouse moors, which are bleak and scrappy with dark stretches of burnt heather and boggy peat. Mum finds plenty to interest her camera lens. Briefly we get a glimpse of a distant skyline of sloping hill crests and edges, and she rattles on about the geometry of the hills. She takes so long changing lenses and cameras that I'm beginning to wish I'd chosen to go with Dad after all, but totally unexpectedly the path over the moors meets the Edge path, and we're suddenly looking down at an amazing view of a reservoir stretched out like a fat blue snake far below us. There are tiny, white cresting waves rippling across it that show it's a living, breathing thing, not just a stretch of still water.

'Stunning!' Mum says. 'Hard to think that two villages are drowned underneath that water. Did you know that? I can't imagine what it must have been like. Most of the families would have been living in that valley for generations.'

'What happened to them?' I imagine the farmers and villagers drowning when the reservoir was flooded. The ghosts of their lives are down there, under the water.

'They would have been given new homes to live in; most likely a lot better than their old ones. It probably used to be just a quiet, deserted valley,' Mum goes on. 'A slow river. A scattering of farms and cottages.'

'I like it the way it is now. This big lake.'

'Oh yes, I agree. It's beautiful. And I suppose the powers that be thought the need for a reservoir was more important than a few farms. We all need water. Great view from up here.' She's already taking the lens cover off her main camera. 'Amazing sky. Look at those clouds, how fast they're moving! And they're so dark! Almost purple, like bruises. Your father might be right about a rainstorm. You saunter on, Carl. I'll catch up.'

Mum loves it when the clouds are like that, full-bellied and already blackening against a sharp blue sky and sunshine. I stride quickly along the cliff path. I can see weird bony outcrops of stones against the skyline ahead of me. I reach the first pile at a run and start to scramble up the rough, slanting rocks. After a bit of slipping and knuckle-grazing, I find my way up to the top. 'King!' I shout. I suppose in ancient times wanderers would have done just that, as if they owned everything they could see, and all the time scanning it for food, shelter, danger. I stand watching the dark clouds gathering along the Edge, like a threatening army. There's definitely rain on the way; I can feel it spitting in the air now. Mum is coming towards me along the path, battling against a sudden fierce wave of wind. She laughs up at me, excited, and I laugh back and half tumble my way down the rocks. I'm excited too. There's something amazing and glorious and primitive about it all, being there among the old rocks in the hurl of the weather. It's not like that in the middle of town, with all the safety of shops and houses around you, like protective castle walls.

'Nature's in charge here!' Mum shouts.

As we draw near the next outcrop of stones, I set off running, arms flapping like a clumsy bird, yelping as the wind snaps the cords of my hood against my face. Again, I scramble up to the top of the boulders, but by now the wind is so strong that I can barely stand upright. I lean into it, arms stretched, letting my weight be held completely. If the wind stops, I'll drop headlong off the edge on to the rocks below.

I cautiously make my way back down towards the track. Mum is walking sideways like a crab towards me, and she puts out her arm and snatches hold of me to steady herself. She can't make herself heard, so she jerks her head to indicate that we should try going round to the lee of the rocks, where it should be a bit calmer. We hunker down, laughing, and settle into our first round of sandwiches.

And then I'm out again, hauling myself up to the top of the stone pile, yelling at Mum to follow me. She won't, I know, for fear of damaging her camera. Suddenly the black clouds open up and rain cascades down, drenching me in an instant. I'm gasping in it as I shimmy down again. We struggle back to the shelter of the rocks and crawl inside as far as we can. It's like being inside an ancient burial mound. I start rummaging in my rucksack to find a bag of crisps, then I pause. I'm suddenly aware of a strange, chilling noise. It's like the voice of someone moaning. It's like a child sobbing.

'Listen to that wind!' Mum laughs. 'It gives me the creeps!'

'It sounds human,' I say, uneasy. There it comes again. It makes the hairs on my neck crawl. It makes my heart cold.

I gulp down the last of my crisps and stuff the bag into my rucksack. 'Let's get going. Rain's practically stopped. Sun's trying to get out.'

'Good. There'll be a rainbow.'

'Photo cliché.'

'Who cares? They sell.' She crawls out after me, fumbling to get her gear ready before the rain comes again. I wander on ahead, glad to be away from those eerie moans and sobs, glad to be out of that dark tomb.

'Have a look at the map, Carl,' Mum shouts. 'There might be a path down to lake level. We can't stay up here. I don't fancy getting soaked like that again.'

I turn my back to the wind and shake out the OS map. It's flapping like a huge, colourful bird in my hands, desperate for take-off. I find Cutthroat Bridge, where we started from. After we crossed the grouse moors, we'd looked down across the reservoir and then we were on the Edge path. I find it now and I trace the length of the Edge with my finger. I can see that all the piles of rocks have names, and I read them out loud. They sound like a rap poem. Whinstone Lee Tor. Hurkling Stones. The Wheel Stones. White Tor. Salt Cellar. Dove Stone. Cakes o'Bread. And then my heart skips a beat. There's a blue kind of fan symbol representing a viewpoint on a hill. Next to it, the words Lost Lad Hillend.

Lost Lad. Al's story!

Mum joins me and peers at the map while I hold it still for her. She traces a path not far from where we are now, leading down to the valley and the reservoir, and the car park where Dad said he would leave the car.

'We'll go down that path. I'll text Dad when I can pick up a signal. We should be able to meet up with him in about an hour.'

I'm wrestling with the wind as I fold up the map. I want to look again at those words. I want to make sure, but I daren't. I must be mistaken. I say nothing to Mum, just push the map into her rucksack. Lost Lad. Lost Lad. So it's true. It's real.

We drop down, away from the wind and all that bluster. It's calm again – the water gleams blue and welcoming down in the valley. We stride on quickly, keen to get there before the rain comes again. But all the time I'm thinking about that cairn, that hill.

Lost Lad Hillend.

I must go there. I have to. But not today. Not with Mum and her camera, and the rain stabbing us like knife points. But soon, I must go there.

HELP ME

THE STORM COMES AGAIN AND NEVER REALLY stops all day. Mum and I meet Dad down by the reservoir and walk back to the car, have a hot drink from the kiosk in the car park and drive to the cottage with the rain streaming down around us. It's as if we're in a boat on a high sea. It rains all night. I lie awake for hours, listening to the water boiling over the stones of the cottage.

I roll over on to my stomach and punch the pillow, and then I hear that sound – that same moaning sound that I heard inside the rocks – and it's coming from outside the cottage. I roll back and sit up in bed, knees hunched, listening. 'It's the wind again,' I tell myself. It's that same chilling human voice. It makes my skin crawl, makes my breath stop still. The moans come louder and louder. They're like pitiful sobs and they're the voice of someone about as old as me. It's no one's voice. It's the wind, surely the wind, muttering around the old stones of the cottage the way it muttered around the stones up on Derwent Edge. The wind, surely the wind.

I lie down and curl on my side with my legs drawn up, pull the quilt closer, cushion the pillow over my head, but I can't drown out that sound of fear, loneliness, grief. And now I can hear words. *Help me.*

'Go away!' I shout. I'm trembling now, and I can't stop. My skin has come loose over my bones; my bones are iron-cold. 'Go away! Leave me alone!'

*

'You were shouting in your sleep last night,' Mum tells me at breakfast.

'Was I?'

'I nearly came in to you, but then you seemed to drop off. Did you have a bad dream?'

'I don't remember.' I stick some bread into the toaster. 'It must have been the wind.'

'No wind,' she says. 'The storm passed over late in the evening, soon after you went to bed.'

I stare at her. 'What do you mean?'

'It was a beautiful night. Calm, lovely. I was outside, looking at the stars. That's when I heard you.' She looks at Dad, biting her lip.

'Carl, we don't have to stay here,' Dad says. 'We can go home any time. You might feel better in your own surroundings.'

'I'm fine.'

'He's fine,' Mum agrees, smiling, relieved. 'We had a great day yesterday, up on the Edge. We both loved it, didn't we, Carl. It was fun.'

'Just tell us,' Dad says again. 'When you want to go home, we'll go.'

I catch a glimpse of my reflection in the mirror over the sink. White face, dark hollows round my eyes, hair lank and sticky. I hardly know myself today. 'Home?' I say bleakly. What is there to go home to? No. I can't leave yet. I have to go to Lost Lad Hillend. 'It's OK. I like it here. I want to stay. I thought I might go over and see Al.'

'Oh, all right.' Mum looks surprised.

'Good idea,' Dad says. 'While you're there, your mum and I will go on a proper shopping spree, in Buxton. I'm right out of beer.'

As soon as they leave the cottage I set off for the farm at a run. I know I have to ask Al to tell me more about the Lost Lad. Did people really see his ghost on the moors? Did he actually know of anyone seeing him? And I'll ask him again about the boy I thought I saw the other night. Was it April, or was it – could it have been – the Lost Lad's ghost?

I really have to know.

LOST LAD HILLEND

APRIL IS STRIDING DOWN THE LANE AHEAD OF ME, her hair hanging in untidy knotted strands down her back. I can hear her humming. She glances back and sees me, and slows her pace so I can catch up with her. She pulls her beanie hat out of her pocket and stuffs it on to her head, tucking her messy hair underneath it.

'How's it goin'?'

'OK.'

'City kids like you get bored out here.'

'It's fine. Mum and I went up on Derwent Edge yesterday, from Cutthroat Bridge.'

'You'll have got a bit wet then.'

'We did. We got caught in the storm. We didn't get as far as Lost Lad Hillend.' I watch her closely. Her eyes flicker briefly, and an amused smile ghosts her lips.

'Oh aye.'

'It was wild up there. We had to shelter in one of those piles of rocks.'

'Like the Lost Lad did,' she says.

I stare at her. I'm completely nonplussed now.

'If you believe it,' she adds.

'Believe what?'

'I suppose you heard him.' She's grinning at me, head on one side, teasing me. She can see she's rattled me. She's enjoying this, but I'm not.

'It keeps the tourists comin'. The drowned villages. Tin Town, where the dam builders lived. The dam busters stuff. The Lost Lad. It's all round here. And there's a memorial stone somewhere to another dog, Tip he's called, who stayed with his dead owner for days. Those stories all get mixed up, you know. And there's no end of plane-crash sites, up on the moors. All that kind of spooky stuff. They're haunted, these hills! The tourists love the place.'

We carry on in silence for a bit. There's that bird again, that skylark, giddy with singing. Will it never stop? It makes me jittery, that restless whistling.

'So you don't believe them?'

'I didn't say that.'

'Why's it on the OS map, Lost Lad Hillend, if it isn't true?'

'Oh, they're all true. Probably. But it's just summat what happened round here. It's local history, isn't it? It belongs to the people who live here. Why does any of it matter to anybody else?'

I shrug. I try to pretend it doesn't matter to me, either. I turn away. 'It's interesting, that's all,' I say cautiously. 'The Lost Lad bit. They say he wanders the moors up there.'

She snorts. 'Who says?'

'Al.'

'He would. He probably tells all the tourists that. Believe it if you want to.'

'I think it's sad, that's all. And interesting.' I deliberately don't choose the word frightening. Don't mention the Lost Lad climbing into my dreams. The voice outside my window. The figure lurking in Mum's photographs. None of that. I would never tell her that.

'And I suppose you've seen him with his dog? Heard him moanin' for help? Soft you are, if you believe that. Soft.'

I'm digging my fists deep into my pockets. I hate her. 'About a week ago,' I say. I force it out. 'I got lost up there, and someone with a dog helped me. It was probably you?'

April walks on, humming again. She's as annoying as that skylark. Then she stops, waiting for me to catch up with her, and I slow my pace, dawdle, tug at long grasses to chew them, and still she waits.

'If you must know, I've seen a dog runnin' wild up there,' she says, when at last I catch up with her. 'Time and again I've seen him. But there's never been a lad with him. Not that I've seen. There's never been no voices. Just a wild dog without a home to go to.'

I still say nothing. My heart's thundering.

It's true, I'm thinking. She knows it's true. But I tell her nothing.

'It gave me a fright once,' she says then.

I wait, heart thumping again. Is she making fun of me?

'I won't go up there on my own now. But if you come with me – if you dare – I'll show you Lost Lad hill.'

I draw in my breath. That's what I want.

'That dog I saw,' she goes on. Her eyes have gone wide and bright. 'I followed him one day. I wanted to know who he belonged to, or was it really a wild dog? It felt like he was leadin' me. He kept runnin' ahead and stoppin', runnin' and stoppin', the way dogs do, as if he was tryin' to tell me summat, show me summat, and I ran after him. And then he did this thing that scared the wits out of me. He stopped by some rocks, and turned round, and he stared at me. Stood stock-still, starin' at me till I was shakin' all over. And then he just disappeared. I don't mean he ran off or crept under the stones or anythin' like that. I mean, he wasn't there any more.'

That's what happened to me, I'm thinking. That night on the moors, when the dog led me home. He just disappeared. But I don't tell her. I've told nobody that.

'You're just saying that. Making it up.'

'You can think what you like.'

She walks off again, and I call after her. 'OK. I'll go with you. I dare.'

'We'll go now then, while Al's at the market. Come on.'

'Now?' Hang on, I'm thinking, this is a bit soon. 'But how? I mean, it's miles away.'

She stands there, humming without a tune, watching me. She's at it again, taunting me. I make myself look at her, but she doesn't have that twist of a smile that makes me feel so vulnerable. In fact, she's the one who's looking vulnerable.

She *wants* me to go with her.

'If you go the way you went, it is. All that way from Cutthroat Bridge. It's miles. But from here, it's just up there. Up that hill. Over the top, and up the next. The way the crow flies. Not much of a map-reader, are you?'

She's taunting me now, challenging me. I could walk away from her and go on my own later. I'd find it. I'd find something. But I'm scared. I need to be with someone. 'All right,' I say. 'Mum and Dad are going to be out all morning. I'll come.'

THE STONES

WE SET OFF AT QUITE A PACE, SHE WITH HER long, easy farmer's strides, me almost at a trot to keep up with her. I keep stopping for breath, staring up at the great beast of a hill stretching away from us, and beyond that, as we climb on up the various levels, the brooding Edge where Mum and I had been. It's tough-going, and I'm out of breath. There's a raven or something croaking over my head.

'It's all weird round here,' I say.

'You mean, no streets, no houses, no traffic. Very weird. Scares you, does it?'

Perhaps I do mean that. Nothing but rolling moors and sandstone Edges, brown tumbling water and sheep, sheep, sheep. And birds. I'm quite uncomfortable here. 'I suppose anything could happen when the weather changes. Especially when there's a snowstorm, in the winter.'

'I should think ghost dogs haunt the moors at any time of year. Why should they just keep it for winter and fog and all that spooky stuff? Why not in broad daylight? Why not in sunshine? Does that scare you? Eh? Do you believe it?'

'Why are you asking me?' I feel wary again. I feel sure she's making fun of me; the innocent townie scared of the dark, scared of voices in the night. 'And you were scared. You told me.' I don't believe now that she's scared of anything.

'I told you. That dog. I used to love walkin' on the Edge there, where them big stones are, where you and your mother went. But not since I saw that dog. I'm used to dogs, I work with 'em, I'm with 'em all the time. No dog has ever scared me before, never. I daren't go up there on my own, like I said. It's not fair. I want 'em back, these hills. I was born round here. They're my special places. I keep startin' to climb up and then summat kind of grabs me. Not a person, not a physical thing. A *feeling*. Makes me skin shiver. No reason. Do you know what I mean?'

I do. The face in the photograph. The shadow. The sobbing in the night. My breathing room. Perhaps she means it after all. Perhaps everyone is scared of something.

'There's a dog,' I say suddenly. 'Down there!' I touch her arm, and she turns round quickly.

'Where?' She's gone pale.

'I can't see it now. It was just running across the hill, quite far down – there!'

'That's a hare!' She almost sounds disappointed. 'A mountain hare. There it goes! And another one!'

I feel stupid. 'I'm sorry. I've never seen one before. Mum would love it.'

'Bring her up here. You'll see loads. Bring her in winter. You'll see ghosts then all right. Ghost hares! They turn white in winter. They're magic creatures; that's what some people say. Al's missus thinks they are. I'd rather see a hare than a ghost dog any day.'

'So that day, when you saw a dog up here and it scared you, is that what you thought it was? A ghost dog?'

She shrugs. 'Possibly.' She carries on walking.

'You know, when I got lost that time – I saw someone and a dog. Was it you?'

'Me?' She doesn't stop. 'You already asked me that.'

'I just wondered.'

'Why would it be me? Anyway. We're here. Head for that cairn.'

We stop when we get to the pile of stones she calls a cairn. I crouch to read a plaque that's been set into it.

'Don't bother,' she says. 'That cairn says nothing about the Lost Lad. It's about the Ramblers Association. But that pile of rocks –' she points to the right of the cairn, on the crest of the hill – 'that's where I think he went. That's where the dog disappeared.'

'D'you think it's the Lost Lad's dog?'

'I don't think anythin', me. But they say the dog lived to a very old age, more'n thirty years. And that he's still wanderin' the moors, or the ghost of him is, and that sometimes he's been seen in the mist, or at night, or in the snow, followin' a shepherd lad. He'll wander for ever. That's what they say round here.'

'That's what Al says.'

'I know.'

I walk right up to the pile of rocks. After a bit she follows me, and when I sit down in front of them, she sits next to me, quiet. We say nothing for ages.

'The Lost Lad,' I say at last. 'So what happened to him?'

'I'm not tellin' you.'

I'm thinking about a boy from long ago, a boy of my age, lost and alone and frightened, desperate, whimpering to himself, *I want to go home.* It could have happened to me.

'Do you?' April asks.

'Do I what?'

'You just said you want to go home.'

I laugh nervously. 'No, I didn't!'

'I *heard* you.' She gets up again and wanders around, looking for handholds so she can scramble up the pile of rocks. I'm unnerved. Has she looked into my thoughts? Had I spoken the words out loud? Or was it the ghost of the Lost Lad we heard, speaking to both of us? I'm spooked, here. *She's* spooking me, that's what it is. I can hear the scrabble of loose stones as she climbs on ahead of me. I'm glad she's gone. It's good to be alone again.

'I'm going now,' I call abruptly to her, and begin to make my way down. She scared me a lot with that ghost dog story. The rocks, the voice, the loneliness of that place – they've all shaken me. I'm feeling a bit dizzy now, giddy with thoughts of foreverness. But as I drop away from those stones towards the valley, I'm feeling better, calmer. I'm not spooked now. I've shaken it off. I like the feel of the sun and the air on my face and the jolt of the earth under my feet as I'm running. I like the long, long stretch of green grass ahead of me. I feel pleased when I hear her panting behind me, trying to catch up. It's as if I'm the leader now. I don't slow down for her. When she reaches me, I drop to a walking pace. It's fine. I'm really fine now.

'Who are you really? How old are you?' I'd never have thought of asking her that before. I don't think I'd have dared.

She laughs, surprised. 'About seventeen. I think.'

'You don't know?'

'Not really.'

'So where do you live when you're not at Al's?'

She puffs her lips out. Maybe she doesn't want to tell me. I don't care.

'I move on to other farms. I walk miles sometimes. I go south, help with hay makin', spud diggin', fruit pickin', whatever's needed.'

'What about school?'

'What about it?'

'But – home?'

'I don't have one,' she says briskly. 'Not now.' Her tone says, don't ask any more questions. And I don't. We split off at the top of the track, saying nothing. She goes on to the farm; I go back to the cottage.

The car's not there, so Mum and Dad aren't back yet. They must be having a great time in a cafe somewhere, catching up on their emails. I'm not sure I like the thought of being in the place on my own. I'll make myself some toast and jam and sit in the yard with it. When I push open the door there's a sudden creaking and rustling on the stairs. A mouse? A bird trapped indoors? That evil farm cat?

A person?

Somebody is there.

'Who is it?' I call out. I can hear my voice shaking.

I go slowly up the stairs. They creak with every step I make. I go into my room; into Mum and Dad's.

I'm almost saying, Jack, is that you? Have you come here after all?

But of course, it's not Jack.

There's no one. Nothing. Of course there isn't. So why is my skin creeping, why is my heart pummelling like fists inside me?

I wish it *was* Jack. I wish he *was* here. Everything would be all right then.

THE MISSED TRAIN

THINK ABOUT THE GOOD TIMES.

I can't.

There's none left.

It's that Ferrari, getting in the way all the time now.

I didn't realise Ferrari was splitting us up until the day Jack missed the train. It was going to be a cracking adventure, and we'd been planning it for days. The idea was this: we'd take our new bikes on the train to Millerton Grange, about fifty miles away, and cycle back along country lanes. We'd take sandwiches and bananas and Mars bars with us, and we'd end up with a bag of chips at the top of Jack's estate.

We arranged to meet outside the station. I was excited; we both were. The Millerton day had come at last! We'd never cycled that far before, never taken our bikes out of town. Jack wasn't there when I arrived at the station, so I hung about a bit and then went into the foyer and bought two tickets. It would save time if he was late. I sat on the cold platform bench and watched the announcements board. The seconds ticked by. I wished I'd arranged to meet him at his house first. I toyed with one of the tickets in my pocket, cleaning my fingernail along the edges. I texted him: *Where are you, bun-head? I've bought your ticket.* No reply. I rang him. No reply. He must be on his way then. Any second, I expected to see him bumping his bike down the stairs and along the platform, red-faced and grinning, shouting excuses before he reached me. I paced up and down, watching the pigeons pecking away at nothing on the concrete. One of Dad's jokes: *We don't get pigeons on our lawn. It's impeccable!*

Our train came in. Commuters streamed off. Hikers streamed on, jostling rucksacks, loud with jokes and plans. The doors closed. The train left. There wouldn't be another for two hours.

I lumped my bike back up the stairs. Still no sign of Jack. I texted him: *Too late, bone-head* and set off back home, then I decided I couldn't face it yet, couldn't face Mum's surprised questions. I decided to go for a spin through the park – I was psyched up for a bike ride (good pun, Dad would have said) and felt too jittery to go straight home. I was fed up and disappointed and angry. Then, on Park Road, I saw his bike propped up against the railings of the Merryday cafe. It was definitely his bike, with a skull and crossbones flag on the handlebars, same as mine. I cycled past, confused, oddly embarrassed, and then I got off my bike and wheeled it back. What the hell was he doing there? It didn't make sense. I peered through the window. And there he was, sitting with Ferrari and his mates, *playing cards.* He was staring at his hand of cards, frowning with concentration. Then Ferrari looked up, caught my eye, and laughed. He nudged Jack. I dodged back, but not before Jack saw me. His face broke into a grin. 'Hi, loser!' he mouthed.

I turned away, swung myself on to my bike and swerved off the pavement, dangerously hurtling into the traffic. I headed straight for the park, bounced up the track towards the ponds and pedalled furiously along the side, actually enjoying the thrill of riding so close to the edge that at any moment I could topple in. When I came down again on to the main track, I saw a bike speeding towards me. I knew it was Jack, but I didn't stop. I swerved around and belted off in the other direction.

'Carl! Carl!' he yelled. He sounded like one of the birds cawing in the trees. Caw! Caw! 'Carl, Carl!'

Let him croak.

*

We avoided each other the next few days, till he tried to make it up. I was walking home on my own after school and he caught up with me. We said nothing, either of us, just loped along side by side. Then it started to rain really heavily, a sudden cloudburst, and we ducked under a tree for a bit of shelter. It wasn't much good, as the leaves weren't out yet. The rain was like snakes, hissing round us. And I decided to have it out with him. It wasn't easy. I told him I couldn't stand those big lads he was hanging round with.

'Especially Ferrari. Ferarri is evil.'

Jack snorted. 'Evil! In what way?'

'He's been done for all kinds of stuff. He steals cars, you flippin' know he does. We saw him! He's a bad lot.' I knew I sounded tame and petty. Jealous even. All the same. 'I hate him,' I said again.

'So do I, kind of.'

'Why d'you hang about with him then?'

'He's a good laugh. He's kind of exciting.'

'Why didn't you come on our bike ride?'

Jack shrugged. He looked hopeless. 'I don't know. He wouldn't let me.' Simple as that. That was it. That was the moment Jack turned away from me. There was nothing, just the rain, the dreary endless rain. Then he muttered, 'We're different, you and me. We're mates, like. We always will be, won't we?' He turned to look at me, and I let the moment hang for a bit. His face looked open and kiddish, as if he was about ten years old.

'Course we will.' I laughed, trying to make light of everything now. It was going to be all right. We'd be OK again. I gave his shoulder a light punch. 'Brothers, we always said. Till death do us part.'

He balled his fists together till the knuckles were white. 'Beyond that,' he said. 'Beyond death.'

He grinned as if it had all been a bit of a joke anyway, and ran out of the tree shelter into the rain, holding up his face to it, opening up his mouth to drink it in. But I felt weird. I felt lost. I felt as if I didn't really know him any more.

RESTLESS

I DON'T LIKE BEING ALONE IN THE COTTAGE, EVEN though I know there's no one there really. It feels creepy. I'm lonely and restless again now. I feel as if I don't belong anywhere.

I loaf back down to the farm and wander towards the yard, watching April working the sheep with the farm dogs. I love those dogs. I can't tell which is which, though one is more white than black, and the other is more black than white. They love people too. When they've worked the sheep through the gate or into the trailer they always run back to April, and she crouches down and pets them. She even lets them lick her face, which I think is pretty disgusting. And they seem to be laughing; you can tell by the brightness in their eyes. I wish we could have a dog.

April finishes the job she's doing – the sheep are streaming away from the closed field gate like maggots, and both the dogs run up to me. It's my turn. 'Good boy!' I say. 'Good girl.' I can't stroke them because of my eczema, and they even seem to understand that. They don't harbour a grudge, just wag their tails and grin up at me, heads cocked to one side.

'Are you scared of *them* too?' April shouts. I can't tell whether she's making fun of me or not. 'They won't bite!' It's as if she's never mentioned her fear of that wild dog she saw on Lost Lad hill. It proves she made it up, just to scare me. There never was a dog up there, wandering for ever, disappearing like a ghost. Daft tale. Daft me, believing her.

So, I'm in a tetchy mood now, and I can't be bothered talking to her. I just turn away and stride up towards the moors again. I'm beginning to know them. They're like a person, telling me a story. I'm walking away from the farm, and the sheep come butting me, baying and baaing and almost pushing me off my feet.

'I'm fed up with sheep,' I say irritably. 'You're so stupid.' And then I'm watching one of the big lambs that didn't get down to the yard; all on its own, it's yelling pathetically for its mum. And I'm remembering another time, me and Jack in a field of sheep, and this was long before Ferrari came on the scene.

Think about the good times.

Nothing to do with Ferrari. Before him.

Think.

The lamb. This had to be the most amazing thing I'd ever seen. It was spring, last year. I was with Jack on a country walk somewhere with Mum and Dad. We were larking about, some way behind them, and we were slamming across fields with our arms outstretched like the wings of a plane, bowing and tipping sideways and weaving round each other, making that bass bee-buzzing sound that sets all your bones vibrating. Sheep were scattering to the right and left of us, and we were pretending they were enemy aircraft. Jack suddenly stopped and said, 'Hey, is something the matter with that sheep?'

It was lying near the track. As we came near to it, it gave a sudden groan and started shuddering violently.

'It's dying,' I said. I giggled. 'You've gunned it down!'

'No, really.'

'Maybe it's having a bad dream.'

'Perhaps we should try and find a farmer.'

I crouched down by it and suddenly I realised what was happening as it half staggered to its feet and started jerking its back end. There, something yellow winked.

'Oh, what?' Jack whispered. I put my hand on his arm.

A black muzzle appeared, then a pair of feet, and then a yellow slithery slippery fishy rush of a thing, a sprawl of jelly, and out came the lamb on to the ground. It was sticky and glistening as if it was coated with syrup. Its mother turned her head and started licking it, lapping like a cat, and shoving it with her nose to make it stand up, till the little bendy thing kicked out its legs and staggered on to its feet. It happened in minutes, but I don't think I breathed at all. We watched in grinning silence as the lamb bleated, flopped over, and struggled to its feet again. I was hugging my knees.

'A little life,' Jack said at last, shy. 'A little animal has been born.'

'And we saw it happen!'

We stood up then and ran to where Mum and Dad had gone.

Dad was coming back towards us, wondering why we were so far behind them.

'There's a lamb! A new lamb!' I shouted.

'It's just been born! We saw it being born!' We were hopping with excitement, now we had someone to share it with.

Mum and Dad came hurrying back to have a look, but by then the lamb was used to being alive, tottering around, trailing its sack of blood with it.

'It took you about twelve months to learn to walk!' Mum laughed. She had her camera out and was snapping away. To Mum, everything is worth a photograph. 'Look how quickly they've bonded. It's wonderful.'

It seemed such a special thing, seeing the birth of a lamb, that I wrote a poem about it. Jack was as proud of it as if he'd written it himself; he even learnt it off by heart. And he put it in for a writing competition at our school. It was weeks later; I'd forgotten all about it by then. He didn't tell me he'd done it till he found out it was shortlisted to win a prize. Everyone was called to assembly to hear the results. I kept punching his backside as we lined up to go into our row.

The main judge was a school governor. He was a tired, frowning sort of man who looked out of place in his special suit. When he came on to the stage in the school hall to announce the winner, my heart was thudding so much I thought I was going to pass out. In that moment, when the judge fiddled with the envelope and took out the piece of paper with the results in it, time stopped moving. I stopped listening. I blew out my cheeks, gasping for air, and Jack nudged me.

'You!' he whispered. 'You've won!'

It was the first time in my life I'd won anything. Maybe I'll be a poet when I grow up, I thought wildly. I'll tramp the hills and write and be invited to places to read my stuff. I had to shake the judge's hand, and it was sweaty like a warm fish. I had to wipe my hand on my trouser seat before I took the prize. I had won a pen – a real fountain pen – it was dark blue with a slim gold band round the cap, and it lived in a padded blue box. I took the prize pen home and polished it, filled it with ink, found a piece of clean paper and wrote my name with it. I had ink all over my knuckles; there were smudges and blots everywhere. I scrubbed my hands and found some fresh paper, wrote out my lamb poem in my best handwriting and gave it to Mum. She said she'd have it framed. I polished the pen again and put it in my sock drawer for safekeeping.

Next day, I sat in class for our English lesson. I was proud and nervous and a bit embarrassed because I knew that Mr Dray was going to congratulate me in front of everyone. What he said was, 'Well done, Carl. I really thought Bethany Wyatt's poem was going to win. Never mind, Bethany, you did an amazing piece of imaginative writing.'

Jack stood up instantly. His face was beetroot-red with indignation. 'But Carl's poem was the best, sir. It *won*. It's brilliant. It's a true poem, we saw that lamb together.'

I never touched the pen again. It's still in its box, somewhere.

POPS

'I'VE ASKED MUM IF YOU CAN COME BACK FOR TEA,' Jack said on the way home. He was trying to make me feel better about that poem, I know.

'What did she say?'

He showed me his phone. *Yes*, his mum had texted. *It's your turn to cook anyway*.

'As long as we don't have lamb,' I said, and we both giggled.

At his house he opened up his yellow recipe notebook, full of grease stains and his scrawly writing. He was a better cook than his mum was and, what's more, he cooked amazing things. We decided to do a risotto. He was main cook, and I did the chopping. We had loud music on so the girls could dance around the kitchen. Grandfather Henry pretended to fall asleep. Pops hovered near us, trying to help. We put him in charge of washing stuff up as we went along. He managed to break a plate and shoved it in the bin, hoping no one would see. We did, but we pretended not to notice. MumRuth did, but just poured herself a glass of wine and went into the living room to read. When it was all ready, Jack sent the girls out to the back yard to pick some flowers and then stuck them in a jar in the middle of the table.

'Ready!' he shouted.

'About time too,' Grandfather Henry muttered. 'And I hope it tastes better than it smells.'

Jack watched us all anxiously as we took the first mouthful. His face was screwed up in anticipation, like those cooks in TV competitions. Grandfather Henry scowled and said it was probably horrible.

'It looks like seaweed,' he muttered.

'Spinach,' I told him, and he shuddered.

'Can't abide the stuff. Never could. Full of grit.'

'Get it down you, Henry,' Pops ordered him. 'It's risotto *fantastico!*'

Grandfather Henry tried a bit and dibbed his tongue on his lips as if he was eating poison. 'Didn't you put any seasoning in this?'

'Not very much.'

'I can taste the not very much.'

'Salt is bad for your heart,' MumRuth murmured.

'I don't care about my heart. I'm eating my tea.'

But good old Pops said it was the best meal he'd ever tasted. 'You could make a living doing this, you two. I hear people in some countries eat insects. Have you thought of having a go at that? Some of those bluebottles on the window look quite tasty.'

'Really?' Jack's eyes were shining with possibilities, though I think he was just sharing the fun with Pops.

'No!' Tamsin and Anna shrieked.

'No, no, a thousand times no!' Mum Ruth said. 'I draw the line at eating insects.'

'Deep-fried and dipped in chocolate,' Pops added mischievously.

'I said no!'

MumRuth and the girls finished the washing up that night, and Jack and I went upstairs to do some woodcarving. I had a set of tools that had belonged to my grandfather, and which Dad kept rolled up in their original green felt pouch, bound with a twist of leather lace from one of his father's own boots. He had held the pouch in both his hands for a moment before he gave it to me. 'Take great care of these tools' he'd said. 'I'd rather you used them in our house but . . .' he lowered his voice, 'your mum wouldn't like the mess.'

We did make a mess. There were wood shavings all over Jack's floor, like little brown fingernails. We tried to catch them on newspapers but every time the door was opened, they wandered over the carpet. So far, I'd made half an owl. It wasn't much good, but I took it down to show Pops, and he turned it over and over in his bumpy veined hands, stroking the only wing that had feathers yet.

'It's rubbish,' I said.

'No, it isn't. It's not perfect, but it's the trying that matters. It was just a block of dead wood, and you're turning it into something that looks alive.'

'Hmm,' I said, not really convinced, but pleased all the same.

'The tree it came from was alive. And you're bringing it

back to life!' he said. 'I can see a real bird in this, Carl, and so can you. Can't you? I can feel it trembling to spread out its wings.'

'You have it,' I said impulsively, but he shook his head.

'You need to hang on to things like this. You grow up so fast and leave stuff behind. But things like this, you want to take them with you. They're special. I hope you finish it one day.'

We all loved Pops.

*

But one day, last November, I had a text from Jack to say that his grandpa had died. *My grandfather has passed away,* he wrote, very formally. He was like that sometimes. I went over to his house immediately, not even finding Mum to tell her. My heart was thumping. I could hear it all the way there. Not Pops, I kept saying. Don't let it be Pops.

The house was in total silence when I arrived. Jack and his sisters were standing like pale statues round the kitchen table, not knowing what to do with themselves or what to say to each other. The cat mewled pathetically round their feet, hungry and ignored. I got his tin of Whiskers out of the fridge and scooped some into his dish, and that seemed to wind the three of them into delayed reaction. Anna burst into tears and ran upstairs to her room. Tamsin turned her beautiful white face towards me. 'Pops is dead,' she whispered. 'Do you know?'

'Oh, not Pops.' I felt gruff and awkward; I didn't know how to look at anyone. 'He's . . . it was like he was my own grandfather.'

Tamsin touched my arm. I wondered if I should hug her. She turned away, sobbing, and followed Anna up the stairs.

Jack sat down at the table, staring in front of him. 'I wonder if he knows.'

'Who?'

'Pops.'

'Knows what?'

'That he's dead. I wonder if he's watching us. He was sitting in that chair, where he always sits. I was sitting here, at the table. I wonder if he thought, right, I'll go now. He just looked at me and said, "It's all right," and then he just slumped his head sideways as if he'd dropped off to sleep. Where did he go?' Jack's voice was hollow and strange.

I felt like crying. My throat had contracted into a lump that wouldn't let me speak or swallow. I wondered whether Jack would cry. I didn't dare ask where Pops was now, where his body was. I looked instinctively at his empty chair, and that cartoon of his on the wall above it; Pops with his red boxing gloves and his woolly hair in his eyes.

Jack shoved his chair back, went over to the fridge and took out a couple of cans of Coke. He pushed one across to me. 'I'm not scared, you know. If you said to me, "Tomorrow you will die—"' he said that dramatically, as if he was on a stage – 'I wouldn't be scared. I'd think, what's it going to be like? I'll find out soon.'

'An awfully big adventure,' I said mechanically.

'You're right. That's exactly right.'

'Peter Pan said that. Not me.' I took a quick swig of Coke and hiccupped. 'It's just words. I'd be scared.'

I heard MumRuth opening the front door and stood up

quickly, leaving the can on the table. 'Come round if you want.'

I didn't know whether to smile or not or what to say when MumRuth came into the kitchen. 'Pops,' I blurted out, and I felt as if I was choking, and she put her arms round me and hugged me. Her face was wet on my cheek. I drew away and pushed past her out of the door, and ran home with fireworks blazing round me, the sky lit with showers of stars, candles for Pops. Hot tears were streaming down my cheeks till I could hardly see. I was crying for Pops, crying for Jack because he wasn't afraid of dying, crying for myself because I was, and I still am.

THE POPS PRESENTS

ABOUT A WEEK LATER, MUMRUTH FOUND AN envelope in one of Pops's drawers. I think she was clearing out his stuff to send to charity. The envelope was addressed to Jack, Tamsin, Anna and Carl. She gave it to Jack, and he looked at the familiar, messy handwriting for ages before he opened it. His hands were shaking. The envelope was stuffed with money. There was a note inside with one of Pops's daft cartoon drawings on the back. Jack turned it over and tried to read the message out loud, but his sniffs got the better of him and he passed it across to Tamsin.

'I reckon you four are the best kids in the world,' she read, in a hushed, solemn voice. 'You've brought me a lot of fun. I hope you have fun spending this someday when I'm not around any more.'

We stared at the money in total silence, and then Tamsin knelt down on the carpet and divided the notes into four equal piles.

'Sparkly shoes,' Anna whispered.

'I can't,' I said to Tamsin.

'He wants you to.'

MumRuth just hugged each of us in turn. 'He always used to say he had four grandkids,' she said. 'He loved you all. Have it, Carl.'

I couldn't believe it. We talked for ages about how we might spend it, and I went home sort of spinning with it all. I ran all the way. It wasn't as if I needed the money, any of it. Mum and Dad gave me anything I wanted, within reason. They didn't heap things on me, but if I said I wanted a particular game or whatever I got it next birthday or Christmas. But a present from Pops was different. I just couldn't decide how to spend it.

'It's not a massive amount,' Dad pointed out. 'It's just something to show you how much you meant to him.'

'How about a camera?' Mum suggested. But then she would.

'I could get a smartphone,' I said. 'Then it would be a camera as well.'

'I think you should choose something to remember Pops by,' Dad said. 'But it's up to you.'

During the night I had a brainwave. I remembered those red boxing gloves hanging in the charity shop, and suddenly I knew I really wanted them – even if I never used them, even if they were just hanging on my bedroom wall. They would always remind me of Pops. It was Saturday the next day, and I went to the shop straight after breakfast. 'Don't let them be gone,' I kept saying to myself. 'Please, please let them be there.'

The tuna-cheeked woman was behind the counter, still reading from her Kindle, still smelling of some kind of flower.

She smiled at me when I went in, recognising me at once. She obviously didn't get many twelve-year-old boys in the shop.

'How's that friend of yours?' she asked. 'How's his violin playing coming on?'

'Awful,' I wanted to say. Instead, I said, 'Pretty good,' and she bunched up her cheeks and beamed at me. 'I knew he'd make good use of it,' she said.

'Those boxing gloves . . .' I muttered. I couldn't see them.

'Ah yes. What happened to them? Ah, I remember now . . . someone asked me to put them on one side for them.' She fished under the counter and there they lay, fists curled like fat red canoes.

'Oh. Right.' It was all I could say.

'You could get some off the internet. Try ebay. I get some lovely stuff there.'

I could afford to buy new ones. But I liked those. I wanted those gloves, more than anything in the world now. It had to be those.

She took off her glasses and flicked through the pages of an exercise book. I turned away, fists in my pockets.

'But that was weeks ago!' she exclaimed. 'Oh, far too long! I'm not keeping them any longer. They're yours, love.'

Mum was so amused by my choice that she said I might as well get the smartphone too. Now I could play games on my phone, send photos, do anything. It was a million times better than my old phone.

'Why don't you get one as well?' I asked Jack. 'We could send each other stuff.'

'I don't want one,' he said. 'I'm going to buy violin lessons.'

I stared at him blankly. It seemed like a waste of money to me, but it was hard to explain why, not without hurting Jack's feelings. 'Don't you want to get something to remember Pops by?' I said. 'Something you can keep?'

'If I learn to play, I can play for ever.'

'Time you put that cat out of its misery,' Grandfather Henry muttered from his corner. Anna giggled.

I remembered what Pops had said about my block of wood that pretended to be half an owl, how he'd turned it over and over in his hands. *It's the trying that matters.* Jack was right. It was the perfect thing to spend his money on.

'What are you getting?' I asked Anna.

'Sparkly shoes. I love sparkly shoes.'

'Oh no you're not,' MumRuth said. 'You'll grow out of them in five minutes and then you'll have nothing to remember him by.'

'I'll keep them for ever,' Anna promised. 'In my box of special things.'

'You haven't got a box of special things.'

'I will have, when I get the shoes. I'll keep the box and cover it with glittery paper and that will be my box of special things.' Eyes like saucers, pleading, and MumRuth sighed. 'We'll see. It's your money.'

Tamsin bought a snake and she called it Bessie, after the grandmother that she'd never met. Pops would have loved that. She let me borrow her sometimes, when Jack was practising his violin, because she felt sorry for me having to sit and listen to it. I was OK really. Jack and I just liked being together. I used to read or play games on my phone, but I liked to have Bessie with me. She was a corn snake, and actually we had no idea whether she was a female or not. She was a beautiful golden-brown and she slinked round my arms like a rope of sand. She ate live mice, whole. The lucky thing about Bessie was that she had no ears, so she didn't have to listen to that fiddle.

After a bit, I realised that Jack was actually making real tunes. I could recognise them, and hum along with them. I even wanted to know how they finished. He was actually beginning to play the fiddle, not just make noises on it.

'It used to be a tree,' I said, still looking at my phone, and I couldn't think why I'd said it, but he stopped playing for a minute and I stopped clicking and we both looked up, hearing something. We almost heard Pops again. His voice. 'You're bringing it back to life.'

'I see him sometimes,' Jack said.

'Who?' I knew who he meant.

'Mum says it's quite normal. Just out of the corner of my eye in the kitchen, I see him in his chair, or on the stairs. I just think I see him. Not a ghost; nothing spooky like that. It's OK, Mum says. It's because he's still warm in my memory, she says.'

THE LONELIEST
MOOR

I FEEL BETTER, THINKING ABOUT THINGS LIKE THAT. Dad was right. It helps to think about the good times, the times before Ferrari stole Jack away. It's fantastic up here on the moors now, the sun beating down – all this air, all this space. It's great. *I* feel great. I'm feeling tons better now.

So I can't understand what happens later.

When I get back home, Mum and Dad are back from their shopping spree in Buxton and Mum is ill with a headache.

'It might be a migraine coming on,' she says. 'I've got those flashing diamond lights behind my eyes.' She looks terrible, not sparkling as she usually is, but pale and quiet and needy, like a sick child.

'Take your tablets,' Dad tells her. 'Dinner can wait.'

'Go to bed,' I order. 'We'll cook.'

Dad throws up his hands in pretend horror as I spill out the contents of the shopping bags and arrange them on the kitchen table. I feel quite excited. Onions. Spinach. Garlic. A carton of passata. Sweet peppers. Polenta. Potted herbs. I squeeze a leaf. 'Coriander,' I say, remembering the pungent smell. 'And this one . . . is basil!' I imagine Jack sniffing it, rubbing a leaf between his fingers. 'We can do this, Dad,' I say. Then casually, grinning, 'You chop. I'll cook.'

'What did you do today?' Dad asks, rolling up his sleeves.

'I went for a walk with April.'

'Oh yes? Who's April?'

He knows perfectly well who she is. As if Mum wouldn't have told him! 'The girl at the farm.' I know what he's thinking. I try to sound casual. 'And before you ask, she's at least seventeen.'

'Too old for you.'

'Exactly.'

We spread the stuff out on the table. 'You're chopping and I'm cooking,' I remind him, in a warning kind of way. This is going to be my show, this.

'Don't let the onions burn,' Dad warns me.

I glare at him. 'Don't cut the peppers too thick.'

He's humming while he chops. Slightly self-conscious, he opens the sound up to a la-la, big and boisterous, the way he does at home sometimes, like a pretend opera singer. The way he used to do, before March 13th. 'Know that tune? You must do! It's the theme from The Dam Busters film. Everyone knows it. I can't get it out of my head since I went to that museum.'

'Never heard of it. Remind me, who were the dam busters?' He doesn't realise I'm humouring him. He loves to tell me things, Dad does. I tip the onions into the heated frying pan, stirring them into the sizzling oil.

'They were an RAF squadron in the Second World War. They used the bouncing bomb on the Ruhr – you must have heard of that? It was designed by a man called Barnes Wallis to bounce along water till it found a dam wall to explode.'

'Oh yes.' I remember the planes we used to make. I remember the model of the Avro Lancaster Bomber, and the stories Pops used to tell us about all the planes. I remember him cradling that other model fighter plane from the First World War in his gentle bony hands; I can hear his voice shaking. 'War wasn't a game; war was for real.' I can see Jack's face, creased with trying not to laugh, and he's red with embarrassment because Pops is so emotional.

'Before they flew in Germany, they needed a long stretch of water between hills to practise in. So they came to the Ladybower Reservoir, where you were walking with Mum. That's where the film was made too. I'll get it off the internet.'

'No internet here, Dad.'

'When we get home. You'll love it.'

Will I? I stop cooking for a moment, tasting the word, *home*. *Will* it be good to be there again – TV, DVDs, films, internet, all that stuff? Everything back to normal. I can't imagine it. What's normal? *Will anything ever be normal again?*

Of course it will. Look at me now, cooking in the kitchen with Dad, Dad singing his head off, like in the old days. He's right. It will happen. It's got to happen. We have to go home at some point. There's another world there, other kids. Reece and

Bryn, they'll let me hang around with them. They're OK. School and stuff. Bessie. Tamsin.

No, we can't stay here for ever.

'It'll be great, won't it?' I say it out loud. 'It'll be great to be home.'

And then my voice is wobbling again, and I'm gripping the handle of the pan so tightly that it's like a vice – I can't loosen my fingers, I can't move my arm.

I can't go home.

I look out of the window. There's golden light on the hill. It's all kind of perfect.

But I don't belong here.

And now I don't feel I belong at home, either.

I let go, finally. I shove the cooking things away. I rub my face with my hands; the smell of herbs is still strong on my fingers. It's too strong. I can't breathe. I can't do this. I can't look at Dad. I can't talk. I stumble out of the kitchen and go up to the bedroom. My room. There's no air inside it. Somebody else has been in and breathed it all away. I pitch myself over to the window and push it open.

There's someone down there, hiding in the trees, staring up at me.

No there isn't.

Go away.

There isn't.

Who is it?

I half close the curtains, but I leave the window open. I need air; I can't breathe. But I stay in my room. Dad knocks gently on my door and I just mutter something and he creeps away again. I can't face anyone. I don't want to eat, or talk, or anything. Later, downstairs, I hear Mum and Dad talking. They must have left the outside door open, because I don't usually hear their voices so clearly. So, the meal has been eaten, Mum's better, I'm still on my bed. I don't know how long I've been there. Hours? I'm staring at moon shadows on the ceiling. My ceiling. I can't sleep, again, again. The stolen air has come back into the room like cold breaths.

'I've got a plan for tomorrow,' I hear Dad say.

'Does it include Carl? I'm not leaving him on his own again,' Mum says.

'Of course it includes him. Mind you, he seems to like spending time with that farm girl. She's an odd one, she is. But yes, of course I want him to come too. It's to do with something we were talking about earlier, actually, while we were cooking the meal.'

'Something upset him, you said.'

'Oh, it wasn't that. Not the Dam Busters! He seemed fine. You know, in a really good mood, like the old days, and then he suddenly went quiet and left everything and went upstairs. I don't know what upset him this time. You know how it is with him these days. One minute he seems to be getting better, and the next minute he goes to pieces.'

I sit up in bed, trying to hear more of this.

'I just don't know what to do for the best. When are we going to get him back again?'

'Soon, Louise. But step by step, in his own time.'

'Did you give him the present?'

'No, I wanted us to give it to him together.'

'Thanks.' Her voice is a bit louder. She must have moved over to the kitchen door. I imagine her leaning against the door jamb, a last cup of coffee or whatever in her hand, gazing out at that amazing silver light. 'He's still not well, you know. He's getting there, but I don't think he's going to be ready for school till the autumn. Sometimes I feel as if I've lost him, as if I'll never get him back again.'

She's closed the door; the voices are muffled. I'm straining to make out the words, but I can't.

So, I'm not well. That's the first time I've actually heard her say that. How much not well? There's nothing physically wrong with me, I know that. I should be fit, with all this walking and fresh air. I'm usually eating everything in sight. So am I going mad? Is that what she means? These voices, these strange figures in photographs, these watchers in the garden. Am I imagining it all?

I throw off the covers and run downstairs, surprising them. Dad has his arms round Mum. She looks as if she's been crying.

'Do you think I'm crazy?' I demand. I can hear my voice, too loud, too cracked. Not like my voice at all.

'What?' Dad laughs, embarrassed. He glances at the kitchen door, realising I must have overheard them. 'Of course not. You're upset, Carl. We're all upset. We know exactly how you feel.'

I stare at him. *Oh no, you don't. You don't know what it's like. You don't know what's inside my head. I'll never be right again. Ever.*

Mum tries to put her arms round me, but I shrug her off. 'You've had an awful shock, Carl. You've been through so much, and it takes time to get over something like that. We think – Doctor Hassan thinks – you're very, very sensitive and upset and you need love and care to help you on your way. But you *will* get better.'

I go and sit down at the table, biting my nails. I'm confused and angry. There's something beating inside my temples, trying to force its way out, trying to break my head open. Mum comes and sits next to me. She puts her arm round my shoulder, and though I tighten up I don't try to pull myself away.

'Carl, you're getting much better. But every now and then you find yourself in a situation where you can't cope, and that's why we think you need a bit longer away from school, away from home.'

'I'm not ill.'

'But you're not well,' she says. 'The doctor said you needed some time away to get better, otherwise you might get worse.'

I remember sitting blankly in the consulting room. I remember a doctor talking to me. I remember I couldn't hear what he was saying because the voice in my head was so much louder than his.

Dad comes and sits opposite us. He stretches his hands towards me as if he wants to touch me but lays them flat on the table instead. 'The suggestion was to take you away for complete rest, exercise, fresh air.' Kind, worried Dad. He's growing a beard while he's here. The stubble is turning white. I've only just noticed. 'Do you remember? You agreed that you'd like that. So we came here for a short break, and we just stayed on. We're in this together, the three of us, for as long as it takes.'

There's a long, slow beat of silence then. *For as long as it takes.*

'Hey, we've bought you a present!' Mum says brightly. 'Well, it's for all of us.'

Dad jumps up and fetches a box, which he pushes towards me. Mum nods at me to open it. Inside is a TV and DVD player and a handful of superhero movies.

'I can't think why we didn't get them before,' Dad says. 'We picked them up in Buxton yesterday.'

'The TV screen's quite big. We can huddle on the settee and watch stuff together,' Mum says. 'Tomorrow night, after that outing you were mentioning, Adrian.'

'Oh yes.' Dad picks up his cue, still bright. 'We're taking you on a walk, up on the moors near Howshaw. We need to drive to the start point. I was chatting to Al down at the farm, about the dam busters actually, and he says there are a few places up there where planes have crashed in the past, and there are bits of one left around somewhere. Not much, because the wreckage is about seventy years old. I just thought Mum would get some interesting photographs there too. Fancy it, Carl?'

I feel dull and tired. I pile up the DVDs neatly. I've watched most of them already, round at Jack's. But they're OK. 'Yes. Thanks.' I try to grin. 'Sounds cool.'

CRASH SITE

S O WE'RE CLIMBING UP TO THIS PLANE-CRASH SITE, and I'm remembering that April mentioned something about wrecked planes when she was doing one of her grouses about tourists intruding on her territory. Dad consults his GPS and points ahead. 'Nearly there.' I'm trying to match his stride but he's panting a bit now and I soon leave him behind. Mum's loitering as usual, pausing to take quick snapshots to remind herself of the route. Her camera is her diary, her journal, her other self, she always says.

I'm loping way ahead of them now. It's not that I want to get there first, I just don't want to keep hanging around dawdling the way they do. And I don't feel much like talking today. I crest the mound of dark moor, which looks completely desolate, breathing mist. The drizzle is like the white curtains some people have over their windows.

I don't know what I'm looking for, then I'm noticing scattered bits of tiny metal, just fragments at first, and now I can make out broken pieces of fuselage poking out of the ground, shards of metal like spearheads. I walk on, following the trail of debris around an area that could be the size of a football pitch. There are simple little wooden crosses stuck in the ground, made out of what look like ice-lolly sticks. Memorials to men who died here over seventy years ago. My stomach is turning over.

Everything's so sad. I don't know what I was expecting, but I didn't know it was going to be like this. I wasn't ready for it at all. Suddenly I can't take it. Suddenly I'm shivering, I'm cold all over. Why have Mum and Dad brought me here, of all places, to see this, of all things?

The mist is drifting like breath. It's spreading damp fingers over my skin, into my mouth, into my eyes. I can hardly see in front of me. Yet there are movements, shapes rising, lumbering towards me, reaching out to me. I can hear sighing, moaning. Desperate, I try to run away, but I can't move.

'Carl? Are you OK?' That's Dad's voice, and I realise I'm lying on the ground. I don't know whether I've stumbled, or thrown myself there, or whether I was pulled down by invisible hands. I grope to my feet, and the mist is thinning and clearing, there's space around me – I can see my parents and the scattered bits of wreckage and the tiny crosses. Dad is crouching over me. I can feel his hand on my shoulder. I press my own hand over his.

'We shouldn't have brought him,' he says. 'Bad idea.'

'Does he take sugar?' I mutter.

'What?'

'Meaning, stop talking *about* me instead of *to* me.'

He stands up, shrugs, blows out his cheeks, helpless. I get up too.

'Sorry, Dad. I'm OK. I just tripped. It's really interesting here.' I'm trying to make it up to them, and I'm blundering in exactly the same way as he is. I want to tell him he can't get it right, however hard he tries, and it's not his fault, he's only Dad. But I can't get the words out. It's weird really, when you think about it. Your brain is saying one thing and your mouth is saying something else entirely.

'I'm OK.'

Of course I'm not. I can't say what's in my head, not to anyone. I can't really talk to anyone.

Mum puts her arms round me. 'All we want is for you to get well again,' she says.

'I know.'

'Whatever it takes, we'll do it.'

'I made a mistake, bringing you here. You used to be really keen on planes, making them and that,' Dad says. 'I thought you'd find it interesting.'

'It is,' I say lightly.

'You had quite a collection, over at Jack's.' We're just strolling round now, while Mum's setting up her cameras. He fishes a chocolate bar out of his pocket and snaps off a row for me. It's rich and smooth, and I let it melt stickily in my mouth. 'You and your collections! I remember your little car collection too!' he laughs. 'It was all you used to talk about. And you used to carry one around with you all the time. What was it now? One of those fancy Italian jobs.'

'I can't remember.' I've tightened up again. Don't say it, Dad. Don't say it.

'Lamborghini! That was it. Your little white Lamborghini.'

THE WHITE
LAMBORGHINI

O K. I'M TRYING TO GET MY HEAD STRAIGHT NOW.
I'm trying to deliberately open up the last few months.
Go there. *Go there.*

So. February the something. This year. I actually saw a
real white Lamborghini parked opposite some posh houses
on Park Road. I was cycling round there on my own, just
enjoying the evening. We'd been for a ride in the woods and
Jack had gone on home. I'd stayed behind to watch some kids
kicking a football around, hoping I'd be invited to join in.
When I saw the Lambo, I hoiked my phone out of my pocket,
nearly dropping it in my excitement. We'd never lost our love
of cars like that, even though we hadn't played with the models
for years.

'Guess what? Get here, quick! A Lamborghini!'

Jack was there in minutes. He threw his bike on the ground
and we sauntered round the car admiring it. More than that –

adoring it, saying nothing, whistling, peering inside it, taking selfies with our phones. We daren't even touch it. It was immaculate. It was beyond beautiful. It was just like the model Lamborghini I loved when I was a little kid, four years old, on my knees, making it prowl. The number plate was DAN 1. Danny, we kept singing. Oh, Danny Boy!

Then we saw Motorhead Ferrari sitting on a low wall opposite, long legs dangling, and he was smirking. He sauntered over to us. 'Like it, do you?' He uses his voice like an American in films, drawling.

Jack blew out his lips and made his loud horse purring sound. I just shrugged.

'It belongs to my uncle Daniel. He lets me drive it sometimes.'

What a liar.

'You mean, he takes you out in it?' Jack said, totally impressed already.

'I mean, he lets me drive it. On my own.' Ferrari made as if to open the door and the car shrieked at him. 'Oh, not this time though!'

A house door over the road opened, a man stood on the doorstep. 'Oi!' he shouted. 'What d'you think you're playing at?'

Ferrari strolled away, whistling.

Jack and I legged it, forgetting our bikes till we were nearly home. When we went back for them, the Lambo had gone. 'Perhaps it was never really there in the first place,' Jack said. 'It was a beautiful phantom.'

'The Ferrari wasn't a phantom though. What was he doing there?'

'Same as us. He likes cars, is all,' Jack said.

I had a quick flashback to that time we saw him hunched up against a tree, in the woods, sobbing. The smashed car, the door flung open, the smell of hot metal. And he had run away from us, even though he was hurt, doubled up in pain, head down, trying to hide his face. 'He stole it, didn't he? That car he wrecked. When we saw him that time in the woods.'

Jack shrugged.

'He's a flippin' maniac. We should have reported it,' I said.

'Grassed on him, you mean?' Jack did that whistle, that annoying trilling whistle. 'It's not what we do, man. Not our scene.' He was drawling. I felt sick. Dusk had fallen; great, black birds were circling round our heads, missing us by fractions. He stopped to watch them. He didn't want to talk about Ferrari, I could tell. I kept ducking involuntarily, but Jack held his ground, daring the birds to scrape his scalp.

But they made me uncomfortable. Everything did. Even Jack. Especially Jack, that night. Him and Ferrari. All I wanted was to get away.

*

And then, over the next few days, I noticed that Julius Ferrari was shadowing Jack at school. It was really obvious. He watched him at break time, standing by him, joking, teasing, occasionally ruffling his hair like a fond uncle. It embarrassed Jack, I knew, and yet I reckon he was pleased with the attention too. I think he was proud to have been picked out. That's when the card playing started, and I wasn't invited round to play with Bessie while he did his violin practice. It was just around the time that we'd missed that train for our day out cycling. So I knew by then that Ferrari had some kind of hold on him, and I hated him for it. Hated them both.

'Coming round to ours?' I asked Jack one day, casual, cool, just trying him. I could see Ferrari coming down the drive with his admirers. So could Jack.

'I'm busy,' Jack said to me. He nodded to Ferrari, grinned, and waited for him.

'Don't bother,' I said. I watched them walk away, the big boys, Ferrari shining in the middle of them like a golden sun. The blond Italian. There's an actor who looks like him – blue-eyed, fake American accent, all that. And doesn't he know it! And then Jack the chosen one trots a few steps behind, till, with a lift of his arm, Julius welcomes him in.

Then came my revenge.

I only did it to get my own back. I wanted Jack to know how it feels, that's all. It was like the time he was seeing Monika Lenski. He just did it for spite. So did I.

One afternoon when I was near the art room, I saw Ferrari coming down the corridor with Jack and some other kids who were currently in favour. They were laughing about something or other, at least Ferrari was smiling in his cool way and Jack and the satellites were giggling, just overdoing it, you know, trying to impress him, and instead of turning away and going off in the other direction I just stood there.

One of Ferrari's car drawings was on the wall opposite me, and I stepped towards it, staring at it as if I couldn't take my eyes off it. Instead of brushing past me like he would usually do,

Ferrari took the bait. He stood behind me and put his hands on my shoulders. I felt sick.

'Like it, do you?'

'It's fantastic,' I said, loud, so Jack would hear. 'It looks so sleek and shiny. Really professional. How do you get it to shine, and make all those reflections and everything? I wish I could draw like that!' I swallowed, hard. Ferrari was almost purring behind me.

'Play your cards right, kid, and I'll teach you.'

The bell went for lessons to start. Ferrari broke away, the crowd around us dispersed, and when I turned round, there was only Jack left in the corridor. He was staring at me, and I couldn't read the expression on his face. Just couldn't read it.

No. Don't go there. Close the door.

Think about the good times.

Dad's right. I must think about the good times, but they keep drifting into this sort of thing, letting in the ghost of Julius Ferrari. I can't shut him out.

I have to let myself remember everything. I have to go there now.

I have to go through that door that takes me to March 13th.

MARCH 13TH

MAYBE HE'D FALLEN OUT OF FAVOUR OR something, but Jack came round that night, as if nothing had happened. He just appeared on the doorstep and Mum sent him up to my room. I heard his steps loping up the stairs and grinned to myself. It felt like a victory. We didn't mention the golden boy and just played some of our favourite computer games, some really rubbish ones, for fun. It was like the old times again. After school next day, we walked back together, talking about Bessie and whether we could get another snake that was just ours. Our steps just happened to drift away from the usual route and up the high street, towards the pet shop.

'We can't buy one though,' Jack said wistfully. 'Not today. We'll just have a look.'

'Just check the price and what's there,' I agreed.

There was a shrill whistle from across the road, and we glanced at each other. My heart sank. We both knew what it was. It was a summons. The traffic was moving slowly, and we were both aware of Ferrari on the opposite pavement, signalling to us. Jack looked across, and so did I, reluctantly. Ferrari was standing with his left palm flat, shaking his right wrist as if he was dealing out cards. Jack shook his head slowly. The traffic closed between us; a bus pulled up. When it moved away again, Ferrari had gone.

'He's a nutter,' was all Jack said.

I said nothing.

That was on March 12th.

On March 13th, we were nearly at my street when a car drew up beside us. The first thing we noticed was that it was a sleek and beautiful classic white open-topped BMW. Cool as ice. The second thing was that Julius Ferrero was driving it. He paused it, leaving the engine purring like a white tiger. And he turned his head towards us, smiling proudly. I tensed. My instinct was to walk away. I had a morbid sense of trouble. I was aware of Jack beside me, willing me to stay with him, to help him. We both thought we knew what Ferrari was going to do. We got it wrong, actually.

'Sorry it's not the Lambo,' he drawled in that lazy fake accent of his. He was looking straight at me. 'You used to love that little toy Lamborghini.'

I was aware of Jack drawing in his breath sharply by my side.

'But my uncle said I could borrow his old Beamer today. Cool, right?'

'Your uncle has expensive taste,' I said dryly. The thing was, even though it wasn't a Lambo, I loved that car he was sitting in. I was trembling to touch it, stroke it, sit inside it. I knew it wasn't his, that he didn't have an uncle who owned cars like this, that no one had given him permission to drive it, that he wasn't even old enough to drive. It was a stolen car. He was underage. No licence. No insurance. He was a criminal. I had my phone in my pocket. I should have phoned the police that minute. I knew all that.

'Get in,' he said. 'I'll take you for a spin.'

He was still talking to me, not Jack. He was still looking at me.

'Come on, Carl. I know you love cars. Beautiful white cars. You have excellent taste. Get in, why don't you?'

I knew exactly what he was doing. He was punishing Jack for spending time with me, for turning down his invitation to a game of cards yesterday. If I stepped into that car, I would become the favoured one. I wouldn't be jeered at, I would be protected, invited to join his group, have the welcoming arm looped across my shoulder, join the card players in the Merryday cafe. I would stand in the sunshine. Jack would be rejected. Jack would be in the shadows.

'Come on, Carl,' Julius said, smiling. 'You'll love this car. She goes like a dream. Just a quick spin.'

It would have been so easy to take that moment of glory, to slide in beside him. It would have been like a dream to sit on those leather seats and glide into the evening. Yet my better sense took hold of me. I stepped away, putting a distance between myself and that temptation.

'Come on,' he drawled again. He ran his hand casually through his silky hair. What a poser.

'No,' I blurted out. 'Get lost, Julius.' I turned my back on him, on that brilliant car, on the ride of my life.

Then: 'I'll come,' said Jack.

I could have stopped him. I could have yanked him out of that magic circle of temptation. But I was mad with him for even offering, for taking my place, for not having the strength of will or the common sense or the distrust or whatever it was that could make him turn away from Julius Motorhead Ferrari. He looked at me for a second, almost asking permission.

I ignored him. 'Yes, take Jack.' I wouldn't look at him. '*He's* your friend, not me. Jack would love to ride with you. Go on, Jack. Get in.'

I walked away, hands deep in my pockets, shimmering inside with anger and a massive helpless feeling of loss. I heard the car purring into life, I felt it humming past me. I didn't look. I had no idea, at that moment, whether Jack was actually in it or not.

I told myself I didn't care.

I took my phone out of my pocket.

NOW

'MORE CHOCOLATE, CARL?'

I feel as if Dad has just woken me from a dream.

He breaks the bar into three and shares it out. Mum's packing away her camera equipment. She looks at me to see if I'm all right and I give her what I hope looks like a smile. I'm enjoying the chocolate anyway.

'It's a gorgeous day now,' she says. 'It would be a shame to go home just yet. Shall we go back to Derwent Edge, where we were so rudely interrupted by rain the other day? I'd love to show Dad those amazing rock formations. What do you think?'

'I'd like that,' Dad says.

'Fine,' I say. I'm only half with them. The memory of March 13th is drifting like smoke around me.

'We might get a bit further this time.'

They walk ahead of me down to the car. Dad's put her camera rucksack on his back, she slips her hand into his, they're chattering and laughing.

I turn back for a moment, scanning the strange, deserted

moor with its gleaming bits of metal glimmering like scattered jewels, and its brave little wooden lolly-stick crosses. The ghosts of the airmen slip back under the grass.

'Sleep tight,' I whisper.

On the far edge, a boy with a dog at his side is watching.

THAT WAS THE DAY

I'M READY TO THINK ABOUT IT NOW. I FOLLOW MUM and Dad, calm, and deliberately allow myself to think about the day when Jack stepped into Julius Ferrero's stolen car.

I had walked away from him as if I didn't care. I felt dumb and listless. I slid my phone back into my pocket. I had dialled 999 and then switched off my phone. Even the temptation to phone the police had gone. What good would it do? Jack and I would never be friends again. Not now. Why take revenge on him?

I didn't go home, but deliberately chose the street up to Jack's estate and walked past his house. The front door was wide open, so I could see right up the hallway passage and into the kitchen, where MumRuth was singing along to something on the radio. She had her back to me, and I could just see Grandfather Henry's feet in his grey felt slippers. Any minute now he would stand up and go and sit at the kitchen table to wait for his tea, drumming his fingers annoyingly on the tabletop. Through the living-room window I could see Tamsin lounging on the settee watching television. I longed to be inside that house, with the comforting smells of cooking and the chatter of television. I hesitated. I could knock, call out, ask for Jack, pretend I didn't even know he was out. I could even sneak up the stairs and wait for him in his room. I could leave a message for him: *That's it, dope-head. Bye.*

Anna came running up the street. She waved, and I lifted my hand and then thrust it deep into my pocket, regretting it. 'I've just posted a birthday card to your mum!' she shouted, laughing. 'I could have saved us a stamp! Are you coming in?'

I shook my head. I felt so miserable that I couldn't find any words for her. She ran into the house and shut the door behind her. The singing stopped. The television chatter stopped.

I trudged on aimlessly. It was bitterly cold, moist, growing dark. I still didn't want to go home. I carried on to school. The gates were closed, no lights on, no cars in the teachers' car park. There was a ghostly, empty, waiting silence. In the distance I heard the wailing sound of a police siren. I walked round the whole block three times, went back up Jack's street, past his house. The curtains were drawn for the night now, there was a warm glow of family inside. I wondered if he was home yet, but couldn't bring myself to knock. I went on up to the woods. Birds were coming in to roost, quivering on to the bare branches. I found our climbing tree and made a half-hearted attempt to haul myself up to the first branch and then lazily slid down again, grazing my hands. I was glad I'd hurt myself. And I just sat on the grass, leaning against the tree, sucking the ooze of blood from my hands, listening to the night coming. A hungry dread was opening up inside my stomach.

Why hadn't I made that phone call? They deserved to get into trouble. Both of them. They deserved anger and punishment. They deserved everything that was coming to them. I took out my phone and called the police. They needed to know. 'Thank you,' was all they said. 'We'll look into it.' I'd given them a false name. I'd said I didn't know who the boys were. Just two kids driving a white car dangerously.

I stayed there until it was completely dark. I'd been out for hours. It was well past midnight. I was numb with cold by then, and hunger was gnawing away at my stomach. At last, I forced myself to go home. I was dragging my feet, counting the lamp posts, counting the cars, anything. I let myself in and Mum hurried downstairs. I think she must have been watching out of the bedroom window for me. Dad came out of the front room. They looked at each other, and the silence was so heavy that I felt I couldn't breathe. They didn't say, 'Where've you been?' 'You're late.' 'We were getting worried about you.' 'Your tea's ruined.'

None of that. Dad said, 'Come and sit down.'

'I want to go upstairs,' I said, but Mum was still on the bottom step, blocking my way.

'We've got something to tell you,' she said.

I didn't want to know.

I think she took my hand. I think she stepped down and led me into the front room and sat me down on the settee and sat next to me, folding my hand in both of hers now as if it was a hurt bird.

Dad went and stood by the black night-time window, his hands behind his back.

'We've got something to tell you,' he said again.

'It's about Jack,' Mum said.

'I know.' I tried to stand up, but Mum eased me down again. I felt weak. My heart was panicking. I wanted to cry. She was still holding my hand. It felt strange, Mum holding my hand like she used to do when I was four years old and we were about to cross the road.

I watched Dad's face. It was different. I realised he wasn't wearing his glasses. His eyes looked strange, tired, hurt, sad.

And then they told me.

But they didn't tell me that Jack had been caught riding in a stolen car.

They didn't tell me that he was down at the police station.

They told me he was dead.

MY FAULT

I DON'T REMEMBER MUCH AFTER MARCH 13TH. I DID go back to school, after a couple of days. Mum thought it was best for me, to help me to pick up a normal life again. We had a special assembly, and our subject teachers said nice things about Jack. Some of them cried. A lot of the girls cried too. Ferrari's lot went into a silent huddle, like white-faced sheep, not knowing where to go or how to behave any more without their sheepdog. It was all right for them. He was still alive, almost, under police guard, I heard, and apparently under deep sedation in hospital. Let him rot there.

Nobody at school said anything to me, and I didn't want them to. There was a special room set aside for anyone who felt they needed someone to talk to, or just to sit and be there away from other people in the classroom. Quite a few girls went up there straight away, clutching each other's hands, smiling at each other in a stricken, sad way. Some of them were hysterical, even if they didn't know Jack. I didn't go to that room. I walked out of the school and went to the park. I stood on the kids' roundabout, trailing one foot on to the ground. Round and round I went. Round and round.

Two weeks later there was a funeral and I said I didn't want to go to it, but Mum said we had to go. 'It's hard for all of us,' she said. 'But we have to go to support Ruth and the girls. Think what it's like for them. They need their special friends around them at a time like this. And it's important for us too. It will bring closure.'

I didn't know what she meant by closure, but when the curtains in the crematorium closed round his coffin, I wanted to rip them open.

After the funeral, I couldn't say anything to MumRuth. My mum had her arm round her and the sisters hovered close to her like pale shadows, but I kept away. Tamsin gave me a ghostly whisper of a smile, and I stared fiercely back at her.

It was as if nothing had changed. Home went on being home, cars moved on the road, birds flew, cats prowled, sun and moon and stars came and went just as they always had done and always will, but there was no Jack. There was no Jack. Jack will never be there again.

Al is right. Nobody thinks about what it's like for the best friend.

I don't know how long after March 13th this happened, a few weeks anyway, but I came in from school one afternoon to find Mum and MumRuth sitting in the kitchen drinking coffee. It almost felt normal. They weren't talking in restrained whispers. There wasn't even a box of tissues on the table. Mum was still sitting near enough to MumRuth to put her arm round her, hold her hand, whatever, but they weren't leaning in towards each other as if one would collapse without the support of the other.

'Are you all right, Carl?' MumRuth asked. She gave me a wispish smile, and her eyes suddenly brimmed. Oh, it was still there then, that river of grief. Of course it was.

'I'm fine,' I said stiffly, awkwardly. I didn't smile back.

I turned away, and Mum said, 'He's lonely, Ruth, but he's coping.'

Coping, is that what it is? Half of me is eating, sleeping, going to school. The other half is turned to ash.

'Come and sit with us,' MumRuth said.

I didn't sit down. I just stood leaning against the counter, doodling with some blobs of water and spilled coffee grains.

'I don't blame Julius,' MumRuth said then. 'I blame the police.'

'The police?' Mum half-laughed. 'They didn't steal the car. They didn't drive out of control.'

'But they did! They were driving far too fast! Why did they have to chase him like that, like a hunted fox?' She gave a shuddering sigh. 'Maybe they didn't know there were two children in that car. How old was Julius? Fifteen? Sixteen? He was just a kid. He was frightened.'

'I think I know what you mean,' Mum said. 'He was only driving too fast because he was trying to get away from the police.'

'It's only natural. If the police hadn't chased him – you've seen them on TV, sirens blazing, lights flashing – this . . . this might never have happened.'

They'd forgotten all about me. I wanted to get out, but I couldn't move, couldn't go upstairs, couldn't go out of the kitchen, or back into the street. Couldn't stop listening.

'You might be right,' Mum was saying. She was moving now, clearing cups away, being busy, the way she always is.

'I know I'm right. Julius would have taken Jack for a spin, showed off a bit, impressed him. Then they'd have abandoned the car in a lane somewhere and caught a bus home or something. Oh, they did wrong, I know that. But they didn't deserve this. This would never have happened if the police hadn't got involved when they did. Don't you agree?'

'Don't, Ruth,' Mum said. 'It happened. It can't be undone. It doesn't help to ask these questions. Don't think this way.'

'I can't help it. I blame the police.'

'It's their job, Ruth. People can't just steal cars and get away with it. Even if they're kids. There's no excuse for theft.'

There was a long, aching silence.

'I wonder who informed them?' MumRuth said into the new silence.

'I imagine it was the owner of the car. He informed them that the car had been stolen, and he had a right to do that. They saw the car, and they gave chase. It's their job.'

MumRuth sighed, that weary, helpless sigh that showed she was tired to the bone, almost too tired to talk. She walked past me to the sink and poured herself some water. It was as if I wasn't there, as if she couldn't see me any more.

'What Julius and Jack did was wrong, I know all that. But if only it hadn't been reported to the police. I can't help it, Louise,

I blame the informer. Jack would still be alive if they hadn't chased after them.'

I couldn't listen to any more. I stumbled out into the hallway and sank on to the stairs. I heard someone whining. It sounded like a dog in pain. Mum came running out of the kitchen and knelt down by me, and then I knew that the whining sound was coming from me.

It was my fault. I rang the police. I did it.

*

I didn't go back to school after that. Mum was at home all day anyway, working on her photographs. I drifted in and out of my room, had my meals, but I wouldn't go out. I just couldn't. Mum and Dad spent a lot of time with me, and that felt strange, but safe. My class teacher sent over some work for me, and Dad said he'd make sure I didn't drop behind. I couldn't concentrate on anything. Mum took me to the doctor, and he suggested that I should see a counsellor or therapist or whatever they call themselves.

If someone had come straight out with the question: 'Is there something you want to talk about? Did you inform the police about the stolen car?' I think I'd have been able to own up, but nobody asked me, not even the therapist Mum took me to see. I went to him for over a month and sat in total silence every time because I couldn't think of anything to say. How could I begin to tell him about the hold Julius had over Jack? How could I tell him I'd handed Jack over to Julius that day? *Take Jack*, I'd said. *Go on, Jack. Get in.* And then phoned the police.

No, I couldn't tell anyone any of that, although it was going over and over in my head. I couldn't say anything. I stared at the therapist's unlikely orange socks and wondered if he bought them himself or whether his wife bought them for him. Really, they were the most interesting thing about him. His favourite words were: 'Take your time, Carl, take your time.' So I did. It was better than being at school anyway; in fact it was quite peaceful. It felt as if the air was snoozing around me. Outside his window I could hear little children playing in the yard; their high squealing sounded like birds. In the end Doctor Hassan of the violent socks suggested to Mum that I needed some time away. That evening she rang Al about his holiday cottage. Dad arranged for a supply teacher, they packed the car with stuff and drove here. I slept all the way, and when I arrived it was like stepping into space. No cars. No streets. No lights. Nothing. Green, green, green.

*

And now, of course, after that episode up on the moors with the dead airmen, Mum and Dad are thinking they've done the wrong thing, bringing me away from home. So I tell them I'm fine, really fine.

'I just went a bit dizzy up there. Not enough breakfast.'

'All you need is time,' Dad says, relieved. 'And there's plenty of that around.'

Time. There you go. That word again. What on earth is time? It stretches out for ever.

Jack's dead. Jack's dead. Your fault. Your fault.

You betrayed him. And so it goes on, day after day. If they look at me, I smile brightly, for their sakes. Sometimes I actually enjoy smiling, because it makes them smile back. Sometimes Dad's jokes are even funny enough to laugh about. Not often. But then, something moves, like the unseen air shifting around me. That white face peering in at the window, that nameless figure lurking in the shadows of the trees. That voice moaning in the rocks. Something whispers to me in the creak of branches, in the flutter of wings, it looms at me like those shapes out on the moor. It's as if a shadowless figure is pacing beside me. And I hear it calling to me. It's always there, more and more often, I'm never without that voice in my head.

Carl. Carl.

Who is it?

Is it the Lost Lad?

Is it Jack?

Let it be Jack.

THE WAY IT
HAPPENED

THIS IS THE WAY I THINK IT WENT, NOW THAT I allow myself to think about it at all. Jack gets into the white car. Superior Ferrari smiles to himself. He nods to Jack and closes his eye in a slow wink, because he's thinking that really this is what Jack wants, that he wants to leave me behind. But he's wrong. He doesn't know Jack. It's not what Jack wants at all. If I'd been in the car as well, it would have been fine. But he sees me walking on, head up, hands in pockets, not looking back. He's willing me to put out my hand, to shout, 'Don't go, Jack. You know better than this.' And when I do, he'll just swing open the door and leap out.

But I don't look back. It looks as if I couldn't care less, that I'll go round to Reece and Bryn or some other friend to spend the evening with. But he knows me. He knows I do care.

And as they round the first corner he's already saying, 'So it's just a quick spin, eh, Julius? Not far?'

Julius doesn't answer.

'The thing is, Carl and I are doing something soon, so I have to get back. I'd forgotten.'

Julius just shows by a tightening of his cheek that he's heard. He drums his fingers on the steering wheel. He takes the car through to top gear, smooth as oil. He's already driving just a little too fast. He swings round the roundabout. The tyres squeal.

Jack shifts uneasily in his seat. 'Fact is, Julius, admit it, this isn't your uncle's car at all, is it? I'm not very happy about being in a stolen car.' I can hear him saying it, see him flexing his fingers, biting his lip slightly. He glances at Julius. 'And you don't have a licence and all that. You're too young. I think I'd like to get out now.'

It's the wrong thing to say, of course, but Jack is incapable of saying anything that isn't on his mind. And Julius smiles and drawls something like, 'Too late, *mon vieux.*' He clicks the play switch on his steering wheel and music blasts out, wild, exciting, loud. He puts his foot down on the accelerator and he's singing, happy and careless.

'Stop!' Jack shouts, and grabs the steering wheel. They're veering all over the road, tyres screeching. They're heading for a wall. They crash.

No, he doesn't do that. That would make it his fault. I change the script.

In this version, Jack knows he can't do anything to make Ferrari stop. He doesn't want to try; it might make things worse. So he closes his eyes, grips the seat as he's flung from side to side. 'Let it be over soon. Let it be over soon,' he keeps saying to himself.

And suddenly he's aware that Julius is laughing, cruel, hard, manic laughter. The car is rocking. He can hear sirens, he opens his eyes, sees the blue flash of a police car, tries to wrest open the door.

'The race is on!' Julius shouts, exuberant. 'You can't catch me!'

And then all the lights of the world go out.

That's the way it happened. I'm sure of it.

A FRIEND OF MINE

I'VE DECIDED I WON'T GO UP THERE AGAIN, UP TO Lost Lad hill. I'm spending a lot of time at the farm now, just kind of mooching round. I like being with the animals; the dogs and the sheep and the chickens. I like their smell and their busyness. Al and April never seem surprised to see me, or pleased, or annoyed; they don't ask any questions. They give me weird jobs to do, like cleaning the lambs' feeding bottles and hosing down machinery. Sometimes I'm mucking out the yard with April. She doesn't say much, and neither do I; we just get on and do the job. I like it like that, and I think she does too. A couple of times she does that weird crow thing, just looking sideways at me with her head cocked, and then she grins and it makes me laugh out loud. And then, at the end of the day, she just strolls off back to the farmhouse and I wander back to the cottage, hungry, tired and satisfied. I eat like a horse and sleep like a log, Mum says. She doesn't know I lie awake often, listening, waiting. The house breathes around me. Out there, up on the dark moor, the hills are watching me.

Then one day, in spite of my resolution, I find myself back at Lost Lad hill, and I don't remember coming here. April's standing next to me, saying nothing. Did we walk up here together? Did I follow her? Did she follow me? I can't remember. I can't remember anything.

'What are you thinking about?' she asks me suddenly.

'A friend of mine.'

'Oh.'

I try to say he's dead. I want to tell her about him, but I can't.

Then I think of Jack in the huge city cemetery where his ashes have been buried. It's like a park, manicured and tidy, with flowers and headstones. And I look down across the full sweep of the hillside, the hares playing below, the birds wheeling above, and I think, I'd rather be here. I'd rather Jack was here. I wish I could bring him.

'I wish he was here,' I say.

'Bring him then.'

We drop back into silence. I could tell her, I'm thinking.

'I'm going soon,' she says suddenly. 'Away from the farm.'

I feel a kind of panic rising up in me. I'm getting used to her odd ways. I think I need her to be here.

'Going? Why? Why now?'

'I don't think I'll be needed for much longer.'

I know it's not true. Al was only telling Dad this morning that he needs every hour of daylight at the moment, there's so much work to do. We hear the tractor long before we get up for breakfast. Most of the lambs will be moving on soon, they've got to be fattened up, injected, herded. I can't imagine his wispy wife helping much. She's so timid, she's really only good for herding Nasty Nellie out of the kitchen. 'Where will you go?' I ask.

She shrugs. 'I suit myself.'

'Home?'

'I told you . . .' she says fiercely.

'You don't get on with your parents?' I can say anything. If she's planning to leave, just like that, I can say anything to her.

'What if I don't have any parents to get on with?' she suggests. That shuts me up.

'Or what if they've chucked me out?'

'You must have someone.'

'Must I?'

I remember Al saying how much they like having April around. She's like a daughter to us, he'd said. We'd love her to stay. But it's not up to me to tell her. It's nothing to do with me.

We split where the track divides, one way to the farm, the other to the cottage. I don't know what she means about going, and whether it will be today, or what. I don't know how to say goodbye, so I don't.

That's another one gone out of my life. I feel as if I'm walking blind now.

I go my way, she goes hers.

THE LOST LAD
CAVE

PILE SOME FOOD ON TO A PLATE AND TAKE IT UP the worn creaky old stairs to my room. Everything is just the same – my bed a jumble of duvet and pillow, my socks and yesterday's T-shirt thrown into a corner, a loop of cable from the socket is charging my iPad so I can listen to music later. Everything the same.

I sit down on my bed with the plate in my hand, and I hear the sound of breathing. I'm alone in the room, yet someone is breathing. Someone is watching me, but no one is there. Someone is so close I could put out my hand and touch them, if they were there. But there's nothing. No one. I'm alone.

'Who is it?' I whisper. 'Tell me. Just tell me. Who are you?'

There it is again, like leaves shivering in a great old tree. Breathing.

I don't know what to do. I'm scared. I can't move. I can't get away from it.

I don't remember whether I ate my tea or not. I don't remember sleeping; maybe I never did. Maybe I was awake all night. When morning comes, I see a plate of sandwiches on the floor. Is that the one I brought upstairs, or did someone else put it there? I don't remember anyone bringing it. I half-eat one, leave it unfinished. I've no idea what time it is. Mum comes in, she says something, I say something, she touches my forehead, closes the curtains, closes the door, goes out. I think I drift into sleep. I wake up suddenly, as if someone called out to me. I can't bear the spacey feeling in my head, the numbness. I make myself stand up. I stumble over to the window and peer out. I see April again by the gate. She's just watching the house, not moving. Then she bends down and picks up a stripey sort of homemade rucksack. She stuffs her hair underneath the navy beanie she likes to wear. Then she turns round and begins to walk away. So that's it? Leaving the farm, as she said she would. Off to nowhere.

I have a sudden need to speak to her. There's something she really needs to know. It's sliding round in my head and jumbled up with thoughts about Jack, and what I did to him. Then the Jack thoughts take over and I don't know what I'm doing any more.

The thing is, Jack is dead, and there's really nothing else for me to think about. Jack's dead, and it's my fault.

You don't let a friend go, just like that.

He wouldn't let me go.

I run down and out to the yard and follow April. It's not a conscious decision. It doesn't occur to me that I should tell anyone I'm going out. I just go outside and run after her. Anyway, she's walking too fast for me. She doesn't hear me when I call out, she doesn't turn her head. Maybe she does hear me. She crosses the fields swiftly and still I follow her, through gates, over stiles, not catching up with her. She strides up the mountain and I stride after her. Her bag looks full and heavy, and she shifts it occasionally. I'm confused now about what I wanted to say to her. Maybe I want to say goodbye – something. Maybe I want to tell her about Jack. Maybe I want to ask her – ask her if she'll write, if I'll ever see her again. Maybe. Why is she letting go of me like this? Maybe she doesn't know I'm here, trailing her steps. Maybe, after all, she does know, and she doesn't care, doesn't want to speak to me.

It doesn't look like her any more. There's a black shape tumbling around her. Is it a dog? I don't know. I can't see anything well enough. It's nearly dusk, the stars are out. Rooks are falling to their roosts in the trees below me. Soon it's almost too dark to see anything clearly. That should tell me how late it is already. It must be nearly midnight. I can't stop now. I can't.

Does she pause, turn, and watch for a moment? I don't know, I can't see her any more. Is she there at all? She's gone. I don't know. I'm not aware of anything. I'm inside my head. I'm inside myself.

By the time I get to the cairn, there's no daylight left. I'm in moon-shadow, but the boulders, the Lost Lad's rocks, are sharp silver. The moon slides away and there's a gap in the rocks like a black mouth of a cave, and I crawl inside, into its cool darkness.

I get as far in as I can, and I curl up in that tiny space and let the silence take hold of me. Now I know what I want to do. I want to bring Jack here.

I'm cold. I'm so very cold. I must have drifted into sleep, and now my shivering has woken me up. I put my hand out and touch only blackness. Is this what it's like? Coldness, darkness, nothingness? Is this what happens after life is over? I curl up.

I think I drift into sleep. I think hours pass. The night goes on for ever. I'm too stiff and cold to move. It's dark, dark, dark, all around me. It's a curtain of darkness.

Silent.

Then it comes. Something shifting in the air, something breathing, something that is nothing, someone who is no one. Or is it me? Is it my own breath I can hear?

I'm afraid. I'm shaking all over, and I can't stop myself. It's growing louder, beating in my head, like heavy wings, making the rocks vibrate, my bones vibrate, as if the whole planet is trembling with it. I'm gasping with fright; I can't drag myself from where I am. I'm locked in this cold cocoon. The air is beating and growling around me. I curl up, protecting myself from whatever it is that is making the world shake. My eyes are shut, my hands are over my ears, and my jaw is clenched tight.

Someone is moaning. *Help me. Help me.*

I know the voice. I know it. It's my own.

Help me.

I'm sorry, Jack. I'm sorry.

'It's all right.' A whisper. It swirls around me, echoes like the sea, the wind, the shift of sand, the whirr of wings.

I'm moaning again. I shove my fist to my mouth. I stifle my sound. I listen.

Softer than breath the whisper comes again. 'It's all right.'

I whisper too, into the darkness. 'Jack?'

'It's all right.'

'Is that you?'

'I've come to tell you, it's all right, Carl. I've come to say goodbye, that's all.'

Nothing else then, only soft, lovely silence. This blanket of peace. I don't want to leave it.

'Goodbye, Jack.'

*

I drift away again, and when I wake up there's a soft grey-green light leaking through from the mouth of the rock cave. I can hear a scrambling sound.

'Carl. Are you awake? Carl?'

I push against the rock, trying to crawl away, or out, I don't know what. Stones skitter under my feet, but my legs are too numb to move.

'Are you all right, Carl?'

I realise now, it's April. She's kneeling beside me, holding my hand, trying to warm me awake.

'Come on out now. You're fine. You're OK.'

I stare at her, bewildered.

'They're all out looking for you,' she says. 'Didn't you hear the helicopter? But I knew you'd be here. It's all right.'

She helps me gently, steadily, towards the light. It's blinding.

It's beautiful. The most beautiful thing I've ever seen.

DON'T GO

MY LEGS ARE STIFF AT FIRST, BUT THEY LOOSEN up as I begin the descent, scrambling a bit, then striding, then running, loping down to the little farm cottage. That lark is singing, and it's a glorious, joyful song. I can even see it tumbling down the green dawn sky.

I suddenly stop and turn. April isn't with me. She's stopped, stooping down to pick up something. It's her stripy rucksack, half hidden under a boulder. She must have left it there when she came to find me.

'Don't go,' I call to her. And then I remember the thing that I wanted to tell her. I have to tell her. I climb back up. 'You don't have to go. You really don't. You need to know something that Al told me.' I frown, trying to get the words right. 'He said that there's always a room for you at the farm. Waiting for you, if you want it. They'd love you to stay with them.'

She just stands there, listening, listening hard, saying nothing.

'You do want it, don't you?'

'I know about that room. It were for their daughter.'

I nod. 'But they don't have a daughter. That was long ago. Now it's for you. You know it is, really.'

She shifts her rucksack awkwardly. It's hanging limply at her side now. 'But I can't just say – can I? I don't know how to ask.'

I have an idea. 'Maybe you don't have to say anything. Maybe you just go down now and walk into their kitchen. You go upstairs and put your rucksack into that room they've got for you. Maybe that's all you have to do, April.'

'It isn't my name,' she says.

'Really?'

'It's just what they call me.'

'Tell them.'

'They call me April, but it isn't my name. My name's Bryony.'

'Tell them.'

She nods. We walk down in silence to the track, and where it divides, we split. I go towards the cottage. I want to see Mum and Dad. More than anything else in the world, I want to see them, I want to tell them it's all right. 'It's all right now,' I want to say, because really, really it is. I'm better, I'm better. I'm better.

I've brought Jack to the hills. He was there in the hollow of the boulders, and it was just us again, and I've left him there. I've let him go.

I'm me again.

I start to run to them. I turn and Bryony is walking fast now. She's running too. She's heading for the farm.

Dad's standing in the yard with his arms wide open, like a

gate. He calls something to Mum, and she comes out of the cottage, and they're both laughing and crying at the same time. I might be too, I can't tell.

Dad folds his arms round me. 'Are you OK?'

'Yes, Dad. I really, really am.'

'You won't do that again?'

'I won't. Ever. I promise.'

He stands back, his hands on my shoulders, and looks me full in the face.

'I promise,' I say again. 'I'm all right.'

'D'you know what? I believe you.'

He's laughing. I'm laughing too.

He hugs me again, and he's too full to say anything else, and so am I. We turn towards the cottage, and Mum.

It's the breakfast of a lifetime, this morning; porridge and eggs and jokes, hot chocolate, toast, more jokes.

'Do you think you'd like a sleep?' Mum says.

I nod lazily. All that excitement and energy is rolling away from me now, in a comfortable, homely way.

'You go up then,' she says. 'And then we'll have a chat about what we do next.'

I pause on the stairs. 'I know what I want to do next,' I say. 'I'd like to speak to Julius Ferrero.'

They look at each other, alarmed.

'I just feel I need to, that's all,' I say. I carry on up the stairs and into my room, that familiar room with its bulging walls and creaking floors. Sunlight is pouring through the windows, filling it with warmth and light. And I know. I know that no one else is there. Nobody watching, breathing, sighing, waiting, moaning. I open the windows. Outside I can hear Al's quad bike purring on the fields. I can see Bryony teasing the dogs, and Al's wife walking across to her. I pull the curtains to, and have the best sleep I've had in my life.

JULIUS FERRARO

I'VE JUST BEEN DOWN TO THE FARM FOR EGGS, AND I chatted to Bryony and Al's wife. Her name is Joanne, and she's really nice. She doesn't look flustered or bewildered or witchy, she looks cheerful and friendly, asks me about school and everything, and I tell her I like school, and I'm looking forward to going back soon, and seeing my friends again. Bryony tells me she's going to market later with Al to buy some new stock. 'They make a great team,' Joanne laughs. 'They'll come home with some bargains, I'm sure.'

As I go back down the track a car passes me and I press myself into the hedge, head down against the swirl of dust. It draws up near the holiday cottage, and I recognise it now as MumRuth's battered old banger. For a moment my heart turns over. I can see Dad and Mum coming across the yard, I can see MumRuth opening the car door and leaning out. They're talking, gesticulating. Mum turns and sees me on the lane, lifts her hand. I start to run forward but Dad meets me at the wall, puts a hand on my shoulder and holds me back.

The passenger door and one of the rear doors open at the same time. From one comes Jack's sister, her hair cropped short now, dyed purple. I grab her name, clutch it in my throat. Tamsin. Beautiful Tamsin.

Anna clambers out after her, grinning with pleasure at seeing me. From the other, a blond boy, his back to me, heaves himself upright on crutches.

'No,' I say, confused, bewildered. 'No. No.'

Not Jack. No. Of course it can't be Jack. He's too tall for Jack. And besides, Jack is dead.

The boy turns round to face me. He unstoops himself. It's Julius. I look from him to Tamsin. Why is Julius Ferrero in Jack's mother's car?

'Mum phoned Ruth from the garage last night,' Dad tells me. 'We thought you might want to see her and the girls again, a nice surprise for you. I think she mentioned what you'd said about seeing Julius sometime soon. But I didn't think they'd bring him with them today. Not here. Not yet. Can you handle this, Carl?'

I'm not sure. Ferrari comes awkwardly round the back of the car and shifts himself towards me on his crutches. He's the ghost of his old self. Most of him looks broken. His face looks broken. He starts crying and nobody touches him, nobody tries to help him. He just stands there crying, and we just watch him. It's a long time before he's able to speak.

'Carl, I want to say something to you.'

I say nothing, only stare at this broken figure. Now that I can see him again, I'm bewildered and confused. He's such a wreck. Does he expect me to attack him? Forgive him? Pity him? Comfort him? I do none of these things. But I'm lost for words. I wanted to see him, I wanted to talk to him, but I'm not quite ready. I haven't thought what to say, what to ask. I'm completely lost for words.

Tamsin comes and stands next to me, as if she wants to give me support. 'He just turned up when we were about to set off this morning,' she whispers. 'He said he needed to talk to you. And you know what Mum's like . . .'

I push past and walk into the cottage, trying to pull my thoughts together. Someone, I think it might even be Tamsin, ushers Julius into the cottage and helps him to sit down at the kitchen table. Mum slips her hand into mine and gives it a squeeze. I could go upstairs, I could go back outside, but I don't. I still can't face him. I stand with my back to him, struggling with myself. I know that he needs to speak to me, and I know I need to listen, but it's hard. So hard. It's the hardest thing I've ever had to do.

'I've been in hospital since . . . since the day,' Julius begins. *Since March 13th.*

In my head, I'm changing his name now. I can't think of him as Ferrari any more. Can't. Won't. He's just a kid, like anyone else. He's just a stupid, snivelling, wreck of a kid. He's Julius Ferrero, a yellow-haired Italian boy who steals cars. A criminal.

'I'm surprised they let you out,' Dad interrupts him. 'I'm surprised you're not in police custody.' I can hear Mum murmur something as if she's trying to calm Dad down.

'Julius has come from the youth court,' MumRuth says. 'He's been granted bail.'

'I suppose you're not likely to run away, not in that condition,' Dad mutters. 'So, what happens next?

'His case will be heard at the Crown Court in two or three months.'

'And what will you be charged with?' Dad asks. It's his teacher's voice. He talks to Julius as if he's a naughty child. I can tell he's just about in control of his anger.

Another pause, then Julius speaks. His voice is like the whimper of a kicked dog. 'Aggravated taking of a vehicle. No licence. No insurance.'

'And . . .?' Dad demands. He pulls up a chair. I imagine him sitting facing Julius, leaning forward, aggressive. 'And . . .?'

A long pause. It's so full of pain that I feel I can touch it, shatter it into shards of glass. Don't, Dad, don't. Don't say it, Julius. Don't say it.

'Causing death by dangerous driving.' Barely a voice there.

Outside in the yard, rooks are squabbling. There's a frenzied scrabble of wings as they take themselves off.

'And you plead?'

'Guilty.'

The long, long sigh. Wind in trees.

'And until you face the Crown Court, you're allowed to go free, do what you like, steal more cars . . .' Dad says.

'If he breaks the conditions of his bail, he'll get a higher sentence,' MumRuth explains. Her voice is shaking. 'As it is . . . I don't know what he'll get.'

'A few years in prison,' Julius whispers. 'That's what I've been told to expect.'

There is complete silence. *A few years locked up away from his friends and family. He's going to lose a few years of his life. Poor Julius. And how many years has Jack lost? He's lost his growing up, his mum, his sisters. He's lost his violin. Me. He's lost his for ever.*

'I wanted to see Carl. I know how he feels; he'll be lost without Jack. Lost.'

I turn slightly then and see how he lifts his hands and drops them again, helpless.

'Actually,' I force myself to say, 'I wanted to see you too. But I never thought you'd come here. Not with Jack's family.'

'My mum wouldn't do it. She said she'd be too upset. So I got a taxi and went to Jack's mother.'

'That was this morning,' MumRuth explained. 'We were just about to set off. Louise had told me you wanted to see him, Carl. It felt like this was the moment. But I had no way of letting you know.'

'There's no signal here,' I mutter, unnecessarily. My mind is racing. It's not helping that Dad is so angry.

'It wasn't easy,' MumRuth says. 'Julius did a brave thing, coming to see me.'

'And then I asked her if I could see Carl, and she said yes, she knows where you are, she'd bring me. I can't believe how kind she's been to me. I know I don't deserve it.' Julius isn't looking at anyone. His head is down, his shoulders hunched. I can see the bones that are his fingers clenching and unclenching on the table, I see them folding over each other like white clam shells.

I glance at Jack's mum, and she nods briefly. I try to understand why she's done it. She must hate him with all her heart, and yet she put him in her car and brought him here because he wanted to see me.

'I don't care about going to prison,' Julius goes on. It's as if he can't hold the words back, now he's opened them up. They aren't the bragging words of the old Ferrari; not his voice, not his fake drawl. His voice is breaking again, and no one puts out a hand to comfort him. He's alone in his world of guilt. 'I don't care what the law does with me, how many years I'll have to serve, where they send me. I just wanted to talk to you about that day.' He's whimpering again now. He's not in control of his voice. 'I want to tell you what happened. If you won't listen, I'll ask Mrs Singer to drive me away and you'll never hear from me again. I promise you that.'

Dad stands up, scraping his chair back on the stone kitchen slabs. 'Carl?' he asks me. His face is blank, hard. He holds out his hand towards me.

I think about it. I think about that day. I had walked away from Jack. I had let him get into the car. I'd let them drive away. I had taken my phone out of my pocket and then I'd replaced it, no call made. I had walked past his house and hadn't told MumRuth that Jack was in a stolen car. I'd walked round the school, into the woods, had tried to climb our tree. And then, then, it was then that I'd phoned the police. I wanted them both to get into trouble. If the police hadn't given chase, this would never have happened. That's what MumRuth had said. My fault. My fault.

It was the right thing to do, I know it was, but I'd done it for the wrong reason. I'd wanted to punish them both.

And I had.

It was my fault.

'Yes,' I say. 'I'll listen.'

'Then I think we should all go outside,' Dad says. 'Leave you two alone together.'

He puts his arm over Tamsin's shoulders. Mum and MumRuth follow them out of the kitchen, into the yard, and close the door.

JULIUS TELLS HIS STORY

HAVE TO LISTEN. JULIUS TELLS HIS STORY, AND I GAZE out of the window as if I'm not listening at all. I don't want to interrupt him. But I'm there, with him, in that white car.

'Every time Jack was out somewhere with me, he talked about you. Especially that night. March 13th. In the car . . . in that white car that night, he kept saying, "I wish Carl was here. I wish he'd come. He'd love it." He wouldn't leave you out. It made me angry. I'm not blaming him. That wasn't what made me crash the car. I drove too fast. It was completely my fault.'

He pauses, shifts about a bit. I can see Tamsin and Anna leaning on the gate, pointing out the lambs. I can hear Jack saying, 'A little life,' that time we saw a lamb being born.

'I've never had a friend like that,' Julius goes on. 'Not like you and Jack. I've never actually had a real friend. Kids hang around me, but they don't like me. I tried to pull you apart. I wanted to. I wanted him for myself. He was a nice kid. He was a sort of brilliant kid, and I thought he was special. I like special things. But I never meant to hurt him.'

I still didn't look at him. I just said, 'So what happened?'

'I was driving too fast, showing off. "Enjoy!" I said to him. "Enjoy the speed." I think he did for a bit. Anyway, he relaxed back into his seat. I thought he had his eyes closed, like he'd given in. Then I saw that he wasn't relaxing at all. He had his phone in his hands and he was bent down, texting something.'

Who was he texting? Had he sent me a message that I never picked up? My mind was spinning.

'That made me really angry. Couldn't he even ride in my car for twenty minutes without texting you? I tried to grab the phone off him, and the car was swerving all over the place. Then I did get hold of it, and I threw it out of the car. We nearly hit a post then, and he yelled at me to stop. It made me laugh, that did. He went completely silent, head down. I drove on and on, further than I meant to. I think I wanted to drive as far away as possible and then dump him, so he'd have to find his own way home. I was so mad at him. We'd left town behind. I hadn't a clue where we were. I put my foot right down, and then I saw a blaze of blue lights close behind me and I knew it was a police car . . . and that's when I panicked. I swung down a lane to nowhere and through a gate and into a field and there was a wall in the way, a great wall looming, and I couldn't stop in time. That noise! That noise as we hit the wall! I thought the whole world had gone up in an explosion. And then silence. I got out of the car; I was running, I was running and I didn't know my back was broken! I felt nothing, just this adrenalin pumping through me. I had to get away. That's all I could think about.'

I'm still saying nothing. I'm watching Mum in the yard now. I'm thinking how tired she looks.

Julius is swallowing hard, building himself up for the rest of the story. He has to tell it. I have to listen. I don't have to look at him.

'I woke up in hospital days later. There was a policeman sitting on one side of my bed and my mother on the other, and she said, 'You killed a boy.' That's how I found out.

'I was in that hospital for weeks, and I had plenty of time to think. My mother came sometimes, but she could hardly talk to me. My father never came, not once. I'm not blaming them. I'm not pitying myself. I was glad of that too. When they released me from the hospital, I was taken to the police station to face charges. My mother came with me, but only because she had to. They might as well have fished a stranger out of their file to come. She didn't look at me, not once. She brought our family solicitor with her. I was told I had the right to say nothing at all once I'd acknowledged my name and date of birth. I was told that I would be interviewed and that there would be three tapes of the interview. One would be kept sealed. One would be a working copy for the police. One would be for my solicitor. I kept nodding. I liked all that.'

Julius looked up at me then, as if he'd suddenly realised that he wasn't talking to himself. 'Can I go on?'

I nod. I've stopped shaking now.

'I was asked to give a complete record of the day of March

13th. My memory was like cotton wool. I understood the questions, but I couldn't find the answers. How did I get the keys of the car? How did I? I don't know. They asked me if I'd stolen a car before. They asked me if I knew that a police helicopter had been following me from half a mile away.

'And then they showed me the video that the police helicopter had taken, and I saw this white car swinging round bends, just missing cars, trucks, bikes, people on crossings. I saw a little kid hauled out of its way. I saw it hurtling through red traffic lights.'

He's sobbing, and I don't want to listen any more. I want to blast out of the room and crash my way upstairs. But I make myself stay. I let him recover, and I'm frightened of breaking up too but I hold on and eventually he carries on talking.

'That message Jack was sending. It wasn't to you. He'd been trying to contact the police.'

I gasp. '*Jack* had?'

Julius looks up at me. His eyes are narrow and dark. 'Does it matter? The owner of the car had seen me taking it. I'd have been caught anyway. I'd still have been followed by the helicopter and chased by a police car, and I'd still have crashed into the wall. He didn't need to tell them. They had me. From the start.'

So they already knew. Long before I'd phoned them, they already knew.

Julius stands up and limps to the door, and I don't help him.

'I just wanted you to know all this. I want you to know I'm sorry. With all my heart. I'm sorry.'

Through the window, I watch him being helped into

MumRuth's car, and then I go outside. The car swings round, and as it passes the gate Julius lifts his head and looks out of the window at me. And I raise my hand.

It's a way of saying: it's over. It's that word, and I understand it now.

Closure.

HOME

TAMSIN AND ANNA ARE STAYING ON FOR THE weekend, top to tail in their sleeping bags on the settee downstairs. It's great showing them the farm and the animals. I introduce them to Bryony and she eyes up Tamsin suspiciously. I know what she's thinking. She's thinking Tamsin's my girlfriend. 'She's like a sister,' I explain. But I'm warm inside.

'More than a sister,' Tamsin says. 'Best friends.'

When we're walking back to the cottage, I tell Tamsin all about Bryony – how she had no home of her own till now, how she could imitate crows, taught me to ride a quad bike, and how she found me the night I had gone into hiding in the rocks. 'She haunted our house too. She used to keep staring through the window at us!' I laugh. 'I thought she was a ghost at first!'

'I think she's nice,' Tamsin said.

'She is. She's great. At first, I thought she was weird, but it was me who was weird. I couldn't tell what was real and what wasn't. She helped me a lot, even if she didn't know she was doing it. I hope we keep in touch.'

'I see.' Tamsin closes her eyes.

'And she's years older than me,' I add. 'She's about seventeen!'

Tamsin slips her hand into mine. We just walk on together, saying nothing, not looking at each other, but her hand is so soft and warm in mine that it's all I can think about. It's unbelievable! How can I be so happy?

We leave it all behind, a couple of days after that. I tell Mum and Dad I'm ready to go home. I really mean it; I'm longing to go. We leave the green fields, the space, the emptiness, the skylark. I go down to the farm and shout goodbye to Bryony over the noise of the sheep in the pen. She waves, then puts her hand in her pocket and pulls out her beanie, stuffs it on her head and grins at me. So it *was* her that night, I think. It was definitely her.

*

Now we're back where the streets are busy, there's noise and bustle, there's the jostle of being at school again, there's homework, and teachers, and new friends, different friends, lots of them. I've got a friend for Bessie too. I call her Nice Nellie, and she stays at my house, but she comes with me when I go round to Tamsin's. We've got a plan. In the autumn we're going back there, Tamsin and me, back to the Derbyshire hills. We're going to take that CD of Pops's, that 'Lark Ascending' one, and we're going to hide it in the Lost Lad cave. That's where Jack is. I know he would have liked that idea.

I had a best friend called Jack. He died earlier this year, and I miss him. I'll never forget him. But there's all kinds of things I want to do now; new, different things, and it's fun. I let go of him that night in the cave of rocks. And he let go of me. We said goodbye to each other.

I've found myself.

JOSEPH

Just me and Bob now.
Moors to usselves, stones and grass and rivers.
Wind and rain and sun and snow, all ours.
Shadows and sunlight and stars, all ours.
We've a story to tell, if anyone wants to listen.

Author's Note

Lost Lad is a hill on Derwent Edge in the Derbyshire Peak District. It is said to be named after a farm boy from the valley below, who got lost in a snowstorm many years ago and took shelter in the hollows between the huge boulders up there. His body was found by a passing shepherd several weeks later.

There is also in the Derwent valley a stone commemorating a dog, Tip, who stayed with his dead master for several weeks and was later found, still alive.

As authors do, I've been inspired by both of these sad stories in creating Joseph and Bob.

Here is their story:

THE LOST LAD

HE LOST LAD, THEY CALL ME. IF THEY SEE ME, THAT is. I hesitate to tell you my tale, in case it gives you fright, but it's a true one, you see. Everyone round these parts knows about me, whether they believe in me or not.

Take a peek at my cottage. Go on in. I don't mind. We're all ghosts now, all the people that ever lived there. It's not much of a place, is it, even now? Ma said her great-grandfather, or someone years before him, built it with stone from the river; some of them round stones that don't fit well together, so the wind can get its fingers through the holes. The floor is flagged and tippety, and there's a great stone fireplace that belches black smoke into the room when the peat's too damp to burn properly. I love that smell, I do, though Ma calls it a right stench.

Pa died when I were only five, so I were used to helping round our little farm even then, and by time I were ten I were doing most of the heavy work. School were in the village, quite a long walk whatever the weather were doing, so I were quite glad to leave it when I were twelve year old.

'Did you not like school then?' Ma asked when I ran home grinning and whooping on my last day, chucking my cap in the air like it were a trapped bird I were setting free.

'I liked doing sums,' I told her. 'And I liked the stories. There was one about me, that the teacher used to tell. Only I had ten brothers in that story.'

'That were never you.'

'Who were it then?'

'That were a Bible Joseph, not a farm boy Joseph. Let me think. He could understand people's dreams, couldn't he? He could tell folks what their dreams meant.'

She fuddled about on the dusty shelf and brought down the heavy family Bible. 'Here –' she handed it to me – 'it's yours now. Find the tale of Joseph and read it to me.'

And that's how we spent our evenings, when the day's work were done: wood chopped, logs stacked, floor swept, sheep fed, lambs looked after; all that done, and I'd pick up the Bible and read to Ma, only I stuttered a bit because the names were strange and like pebbles in my mouth. I had to trace the letters with my fingers.

'You're a good lad, Joseph,' my mother said. 'Your father would be proud of you.'

*

There was just me and Ma. We had a bit of a hill farm, you see 'em scattered over the moors. Only thing that grows there is sheep. It's poor land for grazing, even so. Most of the year it's bogged down with mud, and for the rest it's parched dry and dusty. In spring and summer, you'll hear the curlew and the skylark up there, and there's no grander sound than that. And in the winter, you'll hear the croak of the crow and the rasp of the raven and that's enough to chill your bones when there's no one else to talk to. When I were shepherding up on moors, I might go days or weeks without seeing a soul. I know those moors like I know my dreams. I know the way the wind shrieks across them, the way the rain has such a slant to it that it comes sideways like splinters into your face, the way the drizzlemist breathes like smoke around you. I know the way the snow falls and falls and falls.

I hardly ever saw a living soul after I left school, apart from Ma, the sheep of the fields and the birds of the air, and my dog. Oh, did I not mention him yet? This tale is as much about my black and white dog as it is about me. We bought him as a puppy from the cattle market over in Hope, and we called him Bob because he had a way of bobbing down in front of us as if he were bowing. Then he'd tilt his head and look up, grinning all crafty, panting, waiting for orders.

'By, he's a good'un,' Ma said. 'He wants a master, and that's a good sign in a dog.'

It were true; he were a natural shepherd's dog, like Ma said, and I were a natural shepherd. He just about loved herding sheep, did Bob. He did whatever I told him, as though he knew exactly what I were going to say, like he were alive to every word and whistle. We were that close, like brothers, or best friends, though I never had neither, so how do I know?

'You talk the same language, you two,' Ma used to laugh. 'I have two boys now.'

'I shall teach Bob to read the Bible to you, Ma,' I promised. 'Then I can have a rest.'

I'll tell you more about me and Bob, but that's for later.

There's someone in my cottage right now, another boy. People come and go, stay a while, bring their town things, and leave again. I don't take much notice, I'm only a ghost. But this boy, I sorrow for him. Seems to be my age. Eh, but he's got black worries in his heart and in his dreams, I can tell that. I want to watch him. I hear his grown-ups talking to him and he hardly answers. Hardly hears them. Carl, his name is. I hear them say that to him. He's a bit smaller than me, and his hair's dark and a bit raggedy, like a crow's. He's sad, he is. He's got all those hurts inside him, Carl has. Summat important, that I *can* tell. No one can reach him nor help him, not his mam nor his dad. But happen I can, if he'll let me in.

I followed him one night, on the moors. What if he's lost, that's what I want to know.

'Are yer lost?' I called. I don't rightly know my voice now. I don't know whether I spoke or not. I don't know whether he sees me here or not.

He started to trudge towards me, and I backed off, turned my head away, held up my hand to make him stop right there.

'Take him home, Bob,' I said. That's all.

Now I'm hankering after letting him know about me, the shepherd lad who lived here in this cottage all those years ago, and what happened to me up on the moors. Not the way Farmer Al tells it, scary-like, to give fright for fun. I gaze in at their window sometimes – my window! I like to watch them, cosy in my old house, though the boy doesn't smile much. I like to hear people laugh, I do. I'm in his room sometimes, watching him, looking after him. I mean him no harm. I want to help him. Eh, but is there nowt I can say to the lad to lift him out of his loneliness? You're not on your own, that's what I hanker to say to him. There's all these around you, you must go to them, you must say help me, and they will. You must let them in.

And sometimes he senses me, and shivers, or buries his face under his pillow. It's not me he's afraid of, I think. It's his own self. And he comes up on the moors sometimes, and that's where I live now, this is my home. These rocks, these great stones to hunker inside, these are my stones. Some of them hold my voice still, from all them years ago. Some of them sound like the wind. *I want to go home*. It's my voice he hears here. There's only Carl can hear me, and the girl as comes with him. She knows about me. She understands my story.

MY STORY

LOVED THEM MOORS, BEING UP THERE WITH BOB, training him. He were a canny one, that dog! He had more brains than me. In no time I learned him how to lie down, how to crouch in front of the sheep and make them stop still for him like they were turned to stone till he let them breathe again. You'd laugh to see it. You'd laugh out loud, he were such a canny old buster! He could get them clumped up together to cross streams at just the right place, and if one scuttered away he'd shinny after it a mile or more to bring it back to the fold. And when we were walking 'em over drover's road to market, he'd spot if a stranger's sheep were in the flock and send it scurrying home as if it were nobbut a bag of fleas. He were my dog, all right, through and through. And he loved me so much he would have saved my life, if I'd let him. He tried. It'ud break your heart to know how much he tried.

I were never lonely, once I'd got Bob. When we'd had supper in the evenings, I used to hunker down in front of him and pat him and ruffle his hair all the wrong way, just to make me laugh, and Bob would put a paw on each of my shoulders, clamp, clamp, and make to lick my face. And then he'd be the one as'ud be grinning.

'Eh, give over! You stink!' We'd roll across the floor pretending to fight, but not one of us ever hurt the other. We loved each other, we did. We never wanted to lose each other.

JANUARY SNOW

ANUARY SNOW. THAT'S WHEN MY TALE BEGINS, IF
you want to know it. January. Ma and me, we always think of
it as the month that goes on for ever.

It were a hard, cold day, the day I'm telling you about. Sky
nearly yellow; that meant trouble, I knew that. I were chilled to
my bones even when I were cracking logs for the fire, and when
I came in at the day's end and Ma set me a steaming great pie
on the table, I could have ate the lot, hers and all. She made me
say grace first, even though my nose were twitching, and then
she looks at window and comes out with:

'Eh, Joseph, it's snowing! Would you believe it! I saw no sign
of it coming.' She runs to the door and pulls it open, and the
great sharp flecks start blowing in like moths. 'Eh, and it's bad
out there already! Best get up to the sheep, Joseph, and bring
them down to the home field.'

'Now, Ma? Won't it do after supper?'

'No, now, while there's still some light to see by. It's getting
heavier by the minute. It could last for weeks, this. Just look at

that sky! I'll wrap some pie up for you, and I'll keep the rest hot for when you come back.'

No good arguing, not with Ma. So I fed my feet back into their cold boots and whistled for Bob. He jumped up at once, far keener than I were to go out there into that cold mess.

'Eh, you're a good lad,' Ma said. 'I wish I were fit enough to go misself, but I'm not.'

And I dare say she watched and watched out of the window till it were too dark to see us, and I dare say she busied herself then, packing away the cooking things.

Don't blame her for sending me out on that day. Don't blame her for what happened. She weren't to know.

Eh, but that January snow, it were comin' on that fast into my eyes that I couldn't see out of them. All right for Ma, warm and dry in our house. She'd be dozing in front of the fire by now. I'd half a mind to turn back and go home. 'I'm not doing this, Ma. It in't fit to be out in.' But I carried on, because if I didn't bring the sheep down, who would? And if they didn't come down where they could shelter, they'd die. So I carried on, and Bob kept right beside me, tongue lolling, eyes bright and happy. As long as I were with him, he didn't care what he did. And as long as he were with me, I could keep going.

The higher we climbed, the faster the snow fell, swiping out all the sheep tracks. I ploughed on, head down, eyelids half shut because of the flakes that were grabbing my sight away and stinging my face. I knew I'd have to have faith in Bob's canny sense of smell to lead us where the ewes were hiding themselves, because there were no way as I'd find them by misself. And he must have caught a whiff of scared sheep, because he bounded off sudden, away from my side. I did my best to stumble after him, though half the time my feet were skidding off in different directions.

Well, what happened next? The light dropped, that was what. It were proper night-time. I were in the dark and the snow, and I lost track of Bob. If I hadn't been a grown lad of thirteen, I'd have sobbed for me mam and me bed. I wandered round, whistling, calling, hearing nowt but the creak of the snow under me boots, and I were panicking. I knew these hills like I knew my own house, and yet I were lost. I were cold to me bones that night, and I were frit. I couldn't find me right track, I'd no sense of here or there. I thought, best tek shelter, if you can find somewhere. When light comes, you'll know what's what, and I hunted round for summat, groping, blind, with my hands in front of me. I were that thankful when my hand touched a rock, it could have been my own front door. I felt round. It were a heap of boulders, just right. I crouched down and found a hollow bit that I could crawl into, like it were a little cave. I jammed myself in there, and when my heart had stopped fumbling, I remembered that bit of pie Ma had given me. I'm all right now, I telled meself. And Bob'll find me soon, I know he will.

I didn't fret, not then. I knew Bob would come to me, you see. I tried me best to make that pie of Ma's last me all night, but I kept catching myself nibbling and nibbling at it, it smelt that good, and in the end I give up and wolfed the last of it down. He won't be long, Bob won't.

I strained me eyes to watch, I strained me ears to listen. I clutched my arms round missen and tucked my head down to my knees and waited, and everything around me were coal-black, and the wind even in that shelter were as sharp as fox's teeth. At long last, I must have fell asleep, and I were woke up by a grey light and the croak of a raven far out there. It took me some while to remember where I were, stuck in that hutch of stones. I struggled to shift myself but I were numb all over, and I rubbed me legs and arms till I were fit to move again. I got on to me knees and craned me neck till I could peer outside. That snow out there were as high as me chest, I'm sure of that, and it were blown by the wind into little humps and lumps, like sleeping people. Eh, and it were that eerie quiet!

I whistled and shouted, but there were no sign of my dog. I tried to hoist myself out of the cave I'd made, but me arms was flapping against the sides, it were that slippery. There were nowt to grip on. And where could I go if I got out? How would I move? I'd be smothered.

'Bob, where are yer?' I moaned. I tried to tell myself again that he'd maybe gone home without me, and that Ma would come seeking. 'I'd best stay put and wait.' And I had a laugh, of a sort, because what else could I do but stay put?

And then I had another thought. How would anyone find me if I were huddled inside the stones? I couldn't crouch there with me head stuck up towards the sky all day! I'd soon get buried in it. I pulled back in and found a nice sharp pebble at my feet, and I reached out as far as I could with my arm and swept a shelf of snow from off the boulder above me. I had to twizzle missen round to do it, right hard it were, made me sweat. I cleared it enough to scratch the letters *LOST LAD* on to it. It might not be Ma who come looking for me, I were thinking. It might be a shepherd or a passing tinker who didn't rightly know my name. I thanked the teacher who had taught me to write when I were at school! Then I dropped back down into my cave and frittered the next hour huffing into my hands to warm them up.

BOB

ICANNOT TELL YOU ME JOY WHEN I HEARD A scrunching in the snow, a whimpering and whining, and there was Bob. Bob! He'd found me, he'd sought me out through all that snow and after all those hours, I don't know how long, and there he were pushing himself through into the cave, shaking snow off himself and huddling down next to me. 'Eh, Bob! Bob! Tha's found me!' I shouted, full of hope now. 'I'll keep thee warm, and tha'll keep me warm.'

Oh aye, it were grand to see him. Mebbe I'd rather he led me home or fetched help for me, but right then I just wanted to stroke him. And he wouldn't leave me, not now he'd found me.

Soon, when snow's eased, I'll send him off for help. I told missen that out loud, so's he'd hear me. Soon, I shall. Ma would have realised I must have taken shelter somewhere. Last night she'd have set a candle or a lantern in the window to guide me home, wouldn't she? She'd have built up the fire and sat in front of it, with worry nibbling at her like a mouse at a bit of cheese, and eventually she'd have dropped asleep.

What then, Bob? She's likely to go to the next farm and ask them to help her look for me.

Eh, but think again, Bob, the snow must be deep against her door by now. She'll not be able to open it to get outside. Even if she manages to push it open. No one would hear her, not if she tells at the top of her lungs, and she has a big voice, Ma has.

I were shuddering now. The folks at the farm would have closed their shutters and sealed themselves up against the weather. They would sit it out by the fire, and so must she. 'He'll be all right,' she must be saying to herself. 'He'll have found somewhere to shelter, and there's no coming home in this. He mustn't even try.'

Eh, but it might be three or four weeks before the thaw comes. That's the way it is, sometimes. They have to get out to feed the stock, I'm thinking. Sheep can't get to grass, someone must feed them. Somehow or other the farmers would dig a channel through the snow to get to their sheep and cows. They must. And if they can dig to the animals, they can dig to Ma. They'll help her find her lost lad.

That's what Bob's eyes were telling me. He licked my face, and his breath were warm as sunshine on me cheek.

Sometimes I cried out, help me!

Sometimes I moaned, I want to go home.

Sometimes it were beautiful. It were silent.

I drifted to sleep, and out again, and Bob licked me and gave me comfort, and bit by bit my sleep grew deeper and more beautiful, more beautiful.

More beautiful.

*

That were many years ago. We wander the moors now, me and Bob, night and day, treading with no sound through the purple heather and the golden gorse, listening to the wind round the stones, and the larks and curlews in the sky, and the crafty silence of foxes. We watch the sheep like we always did. We watch the people come and go, and help them if they're lost.

We haunt the hills.

Acknowledgements

With many thanks to five boys from Hope Valley College who talked to me openly about friendship, grief and hurt; to Steve Smith for his advice about police procedure; to my wonderful agents Veronique Baxter and Sara Langham at David Higham Associates who cared so much; to Hazel Holmes and the extraordinary publishing house UCLan Publishing, and the superb artist Tamsin Rosewell and designer Becky Chilcott for creating such a beautiful-looking book, and of course to my husband Billy (Alan Brown) for propping me up, as always!